FOX

FOX FIRES

WYL MENMUIR is a novelist and editor based in Cornwall. His bestselling debut novel, *The Many* (Salt), was longlisted for the 2016 Man Booker Prize. In November 2016, Nightjar Press published a limited-edition chapbook of his story *Rounds* and, in 2017, the National Trust published his story, *In Dark Places*. He has written for Kneehigh Theatre, Radio 4's *Open Book*, the *Guardian* and the *Observer*, and is a regular contributor to the journal *Elementum*. He teaches creative writing at Falmouth University and is co-creator of Cornish writing centre The Writers' Block.

ALSO BY WYL MENMUIR

NOVELS
The Many

FOX FIRES

WYL MENMUIR

SALT

CROMER

PUBLISHED BY SALT PUBLISHING 2021

2 4 6 8 10 9 7 5 3 1

First published in Great Britain in 2021 by
Salt Publishing Ltd
12 Norwich Road, Cromer, Norfolk NR27 0AX United Kingdom

www.saltpublishing.com

Salt Publishing Limited Reg. No. 5293401

A CIP catalogue record for this book is available from the British Library

ISBN 978 1 78463 233 5 (Paperback edition)
ISBN 978 1 78463 234 2 (Electronic edition)

Typeset in Neacademia by Salt Publishing

Printed and bound in Great Britain by Clays Ltd, Elcograf S.p.A

For Em

Fremd bin ich eingezogen,
Fremd zieh' ich wieder aus.
WILHELM MÜLLER, 'Gute Nacht'

In many ways, O resembles the sea more than it does the land.
We live at the mercy of the capricious Meret, and of the light
that filters down to us through shallow waters.
GEORGES FORMEZT, A History of O

PART I

The Wind-up Girl

ONE

W REN LITHGOW ARRIVES in O in the golden haze of late September as the sun is setting behind the mountains of the interior. She observes the approach of the city sprawl from where she sits on a metal lifejacket box bolted to the ferry's deck. Golds shift to red and, in this red glow, the city is all embers.

In many ways, the city state of O looks to her much like any other of the cities in which she has lived. The port is dense with derricks and cranes, with towers of containers. It is busy with stevedores anxious to be home. She tries to make sense of the confusion of buildings that stretches inland, but, beyond the port the hard lines of warehouses and steeples, the sweeping curves of grand buildings on which sit coloured and metallic domes seem impenetrable. In the furthest distance, beyond the city's density, beyond the farms and the fields lined with charming hayricks, the slopes of the mountains, which comprise O's land border, are in silhouette.

The setting sun catches the walls of a building that is taller than all the others, a glass tower that rises far above the rest of the city. Aside from the tower, this could be Antwerp or Rotterdam, Marseille, Athens, Trieste, she thinks. She hopes it might be in some way tangibly different to these other places. She has imagined it often.

She checks her watch. Cleo, her mother, will be, at this

moment, starting her long journey up through the thick layers of tranquillised sleep.

O will be different, she tells herself. She tells herself the same thing about each new place. But it will be different. It will be different because O is the city in which she was conceived, the city in which her father lives, or in which he lived, she does not know which. Her father and O itself, like so much of her mother's past, have always been off limits. She blames Cleo for the first of these taboos, though she can hardly blame her for the second; until a month ago, the borders of O were shut to the world.

Arrangements have been made for their belongings to travel separately. She can picture the process clearly, from the moment the well-groomed man from the removal company arrives at the apartment on Potsdamer Platz. She sees him appraise the uneven steps at the entrance doorway. They will cause the removal team some difficulties, though they are equal to the task. She sees his slight frown at the width of the staircase down which all the furniture must be carried, the tight twist that must be navigated. It causes him to pause, though he does not need a tape measure. He is a professional, after all. She sees him remove his shoes at the door and take out a notebook and pen. He will survey each of the rooms before itemising, wrapping and packing the smaller objects and trinkets. The photographs and concert tickets, creased and faded in their frames, the books from the shelves, the copper-bottom pans her mother insists they should have despite the fact she does not cook, the necklaces and scarves from Cleo's dressing table. Each item wrapped in paper and placed in a small box, labelled, catalogued and stacked with the other small boxes by the door.

4

Later, a team will arrive to move the heavier pieces: the coffee table, her mother's dresser, the Turkish rugs that they will roll and seal and stack in the hallway, the baby grand piano that requires the care of a specialist from the moment it leaves the house to the moment it is unpacked at the new house in O.

Wren is nineteen years old. She is more than half her mother's age. At five foot four inches, she stands an inch taller than her mother, though people who meet them leave with the impression that Cleo is the taller of the two. Wren wears a black trouser suit and over that a black jacket and her dark hair tied back in a ponytail. Around her neck, she wears a pendant, a loose diamond encased in a tiny box of sapphire glass on a long silver chain. The diamond tumbles incessantly as she walks. She feels in many ways she is like this diamond, always moving and never getting anywhere. Against the huge deck, she appears tiny. With her knees up on the box of lifejackets she takes up as little space as possible. She has a slightly rounded face and she bears little resemblance to Cleo who, despite her slightness, fills all spaces and makes herself the centre of them all. From the age of about twelve, men have been assessing Wren against Cleo often vocally and within hearing of both women. Several of them have commented on Wren's peculiar beauty.

It is her eyes, one of Cleo's admirers said before they left Berlin. Or her eyebrows. Or her whole facial structure. So unusual.

When men start to talk like this, Cleo steers the conversation back to music, back to herself, back to safer ground. It is one of the few ways in which she shows her protection for her daughter, though Wren suspects that she does this also to conceal a small jealousy.

Before O, they were in Berlin for three months and they have left under a cloud. It is a cloud of a similar formation to the ones that have followed them from country to country since Wren was a small child.

She has lost count of the places in which they have lived. Each of their moves follows a well-worn pattern. The early days in any new city are filled with expressions of love and of regret for the way things have ended in the city they have just left. Each new start fills Cleo with a sort of fervent light. Each new city represents hope.

Some places they stay for just weeks and others for months but never more than that. London, the place Cleo calls home, is most familiar to Wren, though they have not been there since her uncle fell out of favour. If she adds up the broken months they have spent in other cities, they have lived in Frankfurt, Rome, Paris and Venice for longer. Each move too brief for the even thin roots to take hold. There are places through which they have passed several times briefly: Valletta, Riga, Timisoara, Odessa, and a small island in the Mediterranean, the name of which she has forgotten. Most recently there has been Berlin. At times the cities threaten to merge into a single, nameless metropolis.

The end of things in Berlin was about money. The end of things is almost always about money. Cleo keeps a meticulous list of restaurants and shops in which they can still get credit. Even so, their last days in Berlin felt like an exercise in risk. It seemed to Wren as though they walked along the edge of a cliff. She was aware that in places this cliff was undercut to the point at which it may collapse at any moment and she was unsure exactly where they were safe and where they were in danger of falling through to the rocks beneath. By the time they left, there were so many places, so many people to avoid it had become difficult to keep track of where they were still welcome. To make it worse, she was even more on edge and more distracted than usual.

The cause of this distraction was the prospect of O itself. Wren knows this. She watched her mother's face carefully as she read out the invitation forwarded by Cleo's agent, Anita. The letter was full of the usual flattery. It detailed the many ways in which her presence in O would enrich the city in this year, the first of the new millennium, a year the letter writer referred to as the Year of Hope. There was talk of borders opening and of a grand parade, a chance for the world to rediscover a small corner of Europe that once thrummed to the reverberations of its concert halls and opera houses, and that she, the recipient, the talented and fondly remembered, the much missed and now hurriedly invited, was to be at the vanguard of its rebirth.

At first she said no, they would stay in Berlin and wait for another offer to come through, until Wren revealed the fee. She hoped this news might lift Cleo's mood, though, if anything, it seemed to Wren to send her into a depressive tailspin.

All she said was, Call Anita and tell her they must send an advance.

Cleo takes all her payments in cash. It is a habit she has cultivated over long years of promised money that has never materialised. Once she is paid, she stashes small rolls of bank notes in a wooden box they keep in the living room, which sometimes covers rent and food shopping and other times does not. Some evenings, she takes the money from the box to the casino and leaves Wren alone in their lodgings as she has done since the age Wren began to walk.

Depending on the way the night goes, the next day might be spent shopping in a department store or jeweller's, where Cleo will pick out necklaces and earrings for both of them, clothes, rolls of material, or paintings for the house, and they will eat in the best restaurants. At these times, they make plans. They admire each other in their new clothes and they are the best of friends. If things have gone badly, Cleo will lock herself in her room for days on end or Wren might wake in the night to find her raiding her jewellery box or wardrobe for pieces to sell or to return to the shops from which they were bought only days before.

At Wren's feet is a small case of clothes and essentials. The case contains a few clothes and a small mechanical toy, wrapped in a silk scarf. In her hand, she carries a copy of a battered paperback guidebook to O that she picked up at the Bodemuseum Buchmarkt long before she found out that she and her mother were to move to the city.

Cleo never flies and on the long ferry crossing Wren scanned the pages of the badly produced guidebook. The book's title is O: An Illuminated City. Its binding is disintegrating and many of the pages are missing, though how many pages have already disappeared she has been unable to ascertain as they are not numbered. Those that remain are out of sequence and Wren spent the first few hours of the journey reassembling the book into an order that made sense to her.

O, she read in the guidebook, has been referred to as the Illuminated City since at least the time of Fyador Vary's 1646 text of the same name, a manuscript that is now remembered by title alone. It is a city, according to the author of the guidebook, 'practised in the art of devouring itself'.

It is not just this experience that draws artists to O, the book says, but the quality of the light, a result 'of some indefinable purity of the air that is impossible to measure even with the scientific equipment the city's university has set up around the place in order to quantify what everyone already knows'. She is under no illusion, though: what has attracted her mother is the money on offer.

It is a city beloved of artists, the book claims. Manet holidayed there, she read, and Turner too in later life when his eyes had started to fade. They came, they said, 'to take in the healing light, much as Catholics take in the waters at Lourdes, and to experience the sense of disorientation that is an equal part of O's charm'. Alongside these rhapsodic, floral passages there are a few grainy photographs of monuments and churches, photographs that do nothing to support the central theme of grand illumination, and the book contains no map.

Through the hours in which the few other passengers on the enormous ship slept, and throughout much of the next day, she skimmed through pages of poorly translated character sketches of architects, painters and photographers, through over-wrought descriptions of statues and parks, libraries, monuments and plazas. She checked her pager for messages several times, though there had been none. She mouthed *O'chian* phrases from a page of transliterations to her own skewed reflection in the ferry's scratched windows and felt in the words the unfamiliarity of a language that is nothing like any of those she already speaks: English, Italian, German, French, a little Russian, a little Greek. It depends on Cleo's mood, which of these languages they use. Often, Wren will ask a question in one language and Cleo will respond in a second, with neither willing to switch for the sake of the other.

Wren remains on deck as the ferry passes between the white salt-pillar lighthouses that mark the deep-water passage and is gathered within the outstretched arms of the breakwater. As she watches the city draw closer a thrill runs through her, a sensation that starts in her feet and radiates up through her calves, her thighs, up through her body to her scalp and out through her arms and legs. Whether it is the sub-aural thrumming of the ship's engines that causes this or something else, she does not know, and as the sensation passes through her in great waves, she glad that she is alone on the deck.

It is a sign, she thinks, a sign of welcome from the city in which she was created, some latent recognition from the place in which half of her genes originate. She has imagined this moment countless times, just as she tried to picture the place her father calls, or called, home.

When the tannoy sounds for disembarkation, her mother appears on deck to observe the ship's final approach. Wren stands and joins her and they lean side by side on the railings. The sea below is dark green, bordering on grey, and there is a chop to the waves. When her mother asks to see the guidebook, she passes it to her, though she holds on to the few loose pages for which she has not yet managed to find a home. Cleo looks at the cover briefly. She riffles through the browned pages and drops the book over the side. Wren watches in horror as the covers spread against the white walls of the ferry and when the book hits the water it floats briefly before the loose pages fan out across the surface and are sucked, one by one, into dark water churned white by the propellers.

How dare you, Cleo? she says. Why?

You know I don't like it when you call me Cleo, her mother says. You call me Mother and I'll call you darling.

The book, Wren says. Why?

We'll get you a new one, darling, Cleo says. I've hated that thing for an age. I could smell the mildew on it from here. Anyway, who knows whose fingers have been all over it?

Wren stows the remaining pages in her coat pocket and keeps her hand there for fear she will slap Cleo or push her over the railing after the book. She counts off ten on her fingers and forces her breathing to slow.

Cleo is smiling, though it is a smile Wren does not like. It is a smile that says their friendship is on rocky ground. Cleo has been on edge for days. She does not want to make this trip, though it is the only one on offer. Wren is aware that an argument now could unbalance their arrival, send Cleo spinning off, and there is still, she hopes, a small window in which she might be able to get answers for the questions she has been asking Cleo for years now.

There is a queue in the small customs area. It is not a long queue. Not many people are disembarking. As the ship's crew glide past with their cases on wheels, Wren wonders if there might have been more members of crew than passengers. At a desk, there are two unsmiling customs officials above whom blink closed-circuit television cameras.

The officer asks if they have anything to declare. He wants to know the purpose of their visit. Cleo answers for the two of them. She is here at the invitation of the government. She is here to perform Schubert, Chopin, Debussy, Mahler. The customs officer nods, as though this does not impress him at all, and asks Wren the same question. What is the purpose of your visit? She considers, for a moment, telling him that she is here to find her father, though this is something she has not even revealed to Cleo.

She is accompanying me, Cleo says. That is purpose enough.

The customs official ignores Cleo and turns his attention back to Wren.

You are from here? he says.

She shakes her head.

You are sure?

He is leafing through her passport, looking for evidence that she is mistaken. He paws at each page busy with stamps and signatures, with visas and notations. He wants to know why they have travelled so much. He makes some notes and seems to weigh up letting her through. This is a deliberate tactic. It allows us to perform searches in our databases.

You were born where, then?

London, she says. St Jude's Hospital.

But I was conceived here, she thinks. Again, she wants to say this to the customs officer, though adding any form of complication into the situation would be a mistake, she thinks.

He asks them to put their bags on the desk and Wren can see her mother struggling to keep her temper in check.

He unzips the bags one at a time and puts his hands down the sides and then prods the contents with a finger. He is hardly making a professional job of it, Wren thinks. When his fingers find the hard bulk in the silk scarf and he sees it is a child's toy, he closes the bag again.

Be careful, that dress is Chanel, her mother says, when he opens her case.

The customs officer seems unimpressed by this too. Eventually, after he has looked them up and down several times and prodded through the rest of the contents of their bags, he waves them through.

On the other side of the gates they are met by a driver with a placard on which their family name is written, incorrectly. Lithcow. It is a sign of her sleeping pill hangover that Cleo does not pull him up on the error, Wren thinks. She hates this particular misspelling. The driver is a man in his sixties or perhaps his early seventies. He looks unhappy at having been made to hold the sign, though the arrival of two women seems to brighten his mood a little. As he holds the car door open, he looks Cleo up and down and repeats the process as he does the same for Wren. He says something that sounds to her like shist sees ista obyezevek. Cleo coughs into the collar of her coat.

Wren has said nothing to Cleo since the incident with the book and she does not intend to now.

He approves, Cleo says.

Wren stares out of the window and says nothing.

He approves of you, she continues. He says you're pure O.

Wren can feel the driver watching her in the rear-view mirror and she sinks a little deeper into her seat. Cleo's translation of the driver's words, she knows, is a peace offering though it seems to her a poor exchange for the destruction of her book.

It makes sense, Cleo says a minute or so later, though Wren can tell these words are directed somewhere else and not to her.

She thinks for a moment that Cleo is going to continue,

though it becomes clear she is going to leave it at that. Wren's curiosity gets the better of her and she breaks.

And what's that supposed to mean? Wren says. At that moment the driver puts a hand on the back of the passenger seat head rest, turns and speaks to her again. He talks rapidly and alternates between watching the road and looking back at her. Cleo pays him no more attention. She is watching the city through the window.

Cleo? Wren says. Don't be cruel. Just tell me what he's saying.

He says we shouldn't go out on our own, Cleo says without turning her face from the window. That's what he was saying. He says that it's easy to lose your way. You could end up in the wrong street, the wrong part of town, the wrong side of the wrong river. He said to avoid Zamésche. There are dissidents there. He says that we should avoid coming into contact with the police, and the hospital too, especially the hospital. And that we should observe the curfew. He says we should watch what we say. He should learn to mind his own business.

Her mother translates in the fashion of a child parroting advice given by a worried parent and when she has finished, she directs a short statement to the driver. Wren is surprised at the fluency with which Cleo speaks O'chian. She has always thought that should her mother ever be unable to play piano, she would be able to make a living as a translator, though her lack of patience and diplomacy and, unless it concerns music, concentration might count against her.

Okay, okay, he says. He releases the headrest and mutters something under his breath. Although Wren cannot understand the words, they need little translation.

Though the driver stops talking, he continues to watch

Wren in the mirror. He barely seems to look at the streets. She avoids his wandering eyes and turns her attention to the city. The cars, including the one in which they sit, are ancient and the roads, except for the larger ones, are half-finished, rutted and wide. Through the window, O seems to her like a stage set before the production has started to take shape, before the set has become what it is destined to be. Or one so old that it is fading and disintegrating in places, so much so that the repairs that have been made over the years now constitute the best part of the scenery.

As the car winds its way through the streets, crossing and re-crossing rivers, seemingly with no consistent direction, she winds down the window and inhales the city and the driver continues his monologue. O'chian sounds familiar. It is, she thinks, like a radio that has been set just a few fractions away from a station. She can hear what he is saying and almost make sense of it, though the meaning remains shrouded in static. Every so often she glimpses water and recalls a passage from the guidebook to the effect that each of the great cities of Europe is run through by a great river and O is greater than all of them as it is threaded through by several. One line in particular sticks in her head. 'Any city run through with veins of water is changed by that water, by its mutability, but O's rivers course through it like eels, which remake the city daily.'

TWO

1 166 GYLINCOURTSTRISTE IS a grand house in the middle of a row of grand houses that face the wide, slow waters of the Meret. These houses date back to before the war, by which we do not mean our more recent skirmishes but the second great war during and after which O changed hands several times before being left, once again, to its own devices. These houses are survivors and they are reserved for dignitaries. Most of them have sat empty in recent years and in the week before Wren and Cleo arrive, the rooms are aired, layers of dust removed from the windowsills and kitchen surfaces, and various bugs and recording devices checked, standard practice. Wren observes her mother trying not to be impressed, though even in darkness the house is more imposing and impressive than their apartment in Berlin. Cleo's agent, she knows, will have demanded the best. She appears to have come up trumps here. It is almost a pity, Wren thinks.

The driver carries their bags to the door. He is hurrying now. His air of insouciance has evaporated and he has become brisk, though not so brisk that he does not wait for a tip to appear. Maybe fifteen minutes after they close the door behind them, Wren hears the curfew bells ring.

Cleo takes herself straight to bed. She times her pills to perfection and, even as she arrives, Wren can see her head lolling a little as the sedative takes effect. The beds, she already knows, will be as per instructions, already made, the piano already situated, settled and tuned in the largest reception room. There will be hell to pay if not. All their other belongings remain wrapped in boxes or sit beneath dust sheets.

Wren is still wired from the journey and from the knowledge that she is finally here. Her many years of imagining this place have reached their conclusion. She cannot work out quite how she feels; there are too many emotions jostling for space inside her.

The house is too quiet. There is no traffic noise, no sound of ancient plumbing booming in the walls as there was in the Berlin apartment. There are no curtains at the windows yet either and the thick blanket-like quality of the dark beyond them unsettles her. It feels unnatural to be in a city and for there not to be light, movement, a constant background hum. Though she can only see her own reflection in the front room window, she feels she is being observed from outside and retreats.

She opens her bag, the one she packed on the bed of the apartment in Potsdamer Platz. The first thing she unwraps is the object in the silk scarf and lays the small, articulated figure of a girl in a grey, hooded coat on the bedcover. This toy has been with her since she turned twelve. On the night of Wren's twelfth birthday Cleo had returned home late, long after the concert hall had shut its doors. Wren had listened as she crashed about in the kitchen. When Cleo appeared at her door, Wren watched her through almost-closed eyes. She could see by the way her mother propped herself in the doorway that she was drunk. She was holding a small bundle, which she threw onto Wren's bed before leaving and when she was gone Wren near as leapt up to see what it was. It was wrapped in a silk scarf of the sort her mother often wore and she unwrapped the package on the bed as carefully as any archaeologist might unwind a mummy from the tomb of a pharaoh.

She's the only thing, her mother said when she asked about it the next morning, aside from you, that I took away from the city in which you were conceived. She belonged to your father.

It was a rare moment of openness and Wren listened hard, barely daring to move or breathe. This was the first time Cleo had mentioned her father and she was unsure how to react, any information about her father having been forbidden until then. She was unsure too, at this time, what it meant to be conceived, though she held onto these words in the way that a child starved of attention will remember a hug or a brief moment of connection. Even at this age it surprised Wren that her mother had kept the wind-up girl. Her mother disliked anything childish. Wren asked her if the wind-up girl had a name and Cleo said no, there was no point naming something that is not a person. All the same, Wren named her Ariadne after the girl in a story her uncle had told her on their last visit to London.

Ariadne is unlike the other things in Wren's life. She is unmanicured, plain and heavy. When Ariadne came to her, she carried her own key on a thin cotton belt around her waist. Her keyhole is accessed through a slit in the side of her grey coat. Ariadne wears a dark robe with a hood that can be pulled up over her head and which, when it is raised, masks her face entirely. On her underside, she has several tiny wheels. Beneath her robe, her wooden body has been polished smooth by the touch of countless hands; there is a case around a hidden mechanism, and she feels far heavier than she looks. Wren picks her up from the bedcover and holds her for a minute. This is part of a ritual she has perfected over a long time. Ariadne has an unusual weight, as though she is dense in a way that is somehow too great for the small frame. Her face is serious, the small line of her mouth a tight half-smile.

Sometimes, Cleo would leave her on her own for days at a time. She never explained where she was going and she sent Wren no messages as to when she would be back. Wren learned to live off what little money was in the wooden box, or on the credit they had in various shops where her mother was well known. When Cleo returned from these absences, it was often with armfuls of gifts, things Wren neither wanted nor understood, and promises that Cleo would never leave her daughter alone in a strange city again. Other times, Cleo returned empty-handed and locked herself in her room. In some ways, this was worse than when she was not there, a worse kind of alone. Cleo referred to her variously as her precious, her everything, and her burden, and the feeling Wren was left with as she grew older was that she was loved at times, tolerated at others, and always costly.

During long hours in which her mother was away, Wren would set Ariadne on the floor and wind her mechanism. Ariadne seemed so simple that the complexity of her movements always surprised her. Wren was convinced that Ariadne moved with purpose, as though she was working her way through a maze. Wren would sketch her movements on paper, though Ariadne appeared never to repeat the same pattern and Wren could make no sense of her. It was as though, each time Wren wound her mechanism, Ariadne picked up where she had left off. At night, Wren dreamt that the girl took her by the hand and led her to her father, who was waiting for her, hidden in a city she had never visited.

During one of their many moves, Wren lost Ariadne's key.

The belt around the wind-up girl's waist frayed and snapped or fell from her. She searched for it every day for weeks after, frantic at its loss, but the key was gone. Wren is careless, as her mother has often told her, and now, when she lifts Ariadne, she can hear her mechanism tumbling inside her. She is a beautiful, broken thing.

THREE

I WANT YOU to tell me about him, Wren says the next morning.

Cleo is unfolding clothes on the bed in her room.

Who?

She knows who.

You know who, Wren says. My father. Now we're here, I want to know more.

I'm due in rehearsal, Cleo replies.

She holds up two dresses.

This one or this?

She is not really asking Wren; it is just for show.

I want to know about him. Anything.

There's nothing to tell, she says. The black one. Obviously the black one.

Cleo is certain about everything. It is what makes her successful, she says. If you are uncertain in your own mind, everyone will be able to tell, and they will know you are faking it. It is as true in music as it is in life, she says.

Wren hears a car pull up outside and when she looks out of the window the driver waves up at her as if they are old friends. She does not wave back. He strikes her as the sort of man of the kind it would not do to encourage his attentions.

The car will bring me back later tonight, Cleo says as she walks towards the door. Promise. You settle in, and then later on we'll make it a proper home.

Where are you rehearsing? Wren asks.

I'll find out when I arrive, I imagine, Cleo says. Don't leave the house until I get back.

She picks up her bag and a folder of sheet music and swings out of the house. If she has any sense of what Wren is about to do next, she shows no sign of it.

The door slams behind her and the house is empty again.

Wren has planned this moment for years, though there are things she needs to do first. She owes her mother this much at least. Her role is one that has been established over many relocations. She will arrange and rearrange the furniture until the new house resembles the last as closely as possible: the photographs in the hallway in the same order, the pictures at the same level and distributed in the same way in each of the rooms, the cushions and throws on the sofas, the same items in the same order in the same drawers. It is one of the few things she knows she can do to keep Cleo's moods in check.

She wears black leggings and a black t-shirt that is long enough to pass for a dress and her feet are bare on the carpet, her toes buried in the thick pile as she hangs photographs in the entrance hall. Her jewellery is silver: plain rings, stud earrings and the necklace with the pendant.

She struggles to shift heavy chests of drawers in rooms in which the ceilings feel too high. She hangs mirrors and unpacks the contents of the kitchen into the drawers and she disposes of chipped and marked plates and glasses. Rome, London, Berlin – these are dreamlike, uncertain places to her now, superficial. Her memories of Berlin are fading already and though she has been in O only a matter of hours it already seems to her to possess substance that other cities lack.

When she is almost done, she stands in front of the

kaleidoscope of paintings, photographs, framed posters and tickets that she has recreated on the walls of the hallway. There are mostly portraits of people she has never met, faces from a glittering past that is her mother's alone, parties and awards ceremonies, concerts and dinners, posters for recitals, some scrawled over with signatures and messages: È *stato stupendo*; *Моје срце куца само за тебе*; Brava, you were marvellous, the finest we've had. She knows these photographs better than most people know the details of a single treasured possession or a painting that has been passed down through generations. Almost everything in the house belongs to her mother. Beautiful, weighty things she has collected over a lifetime, a life to which Wren has only ever been partly connected. Visitors stop in the hallway to take in the framed patchwork of people and events and it is often ten or fifteen minutes before they progress further.

There are also, among the others, photographs in which Wren features. She barely recognises herself in these images and the overwhelming sense she has when she looks at them is that Cleo's life was infinitely richer before Wren was born. Most of the photographs feature Cleo, impossibly glamorous at the piano, her long neck and the softness of her back exposed by the fall of her dress. In some of these photographs, with her fingers stretched across the keys, she is entirely lost to the music, the expression Wren knows best of all. Others show her in the company of people who also wear their beauty lightly and whose outfits and demeanour match the grandiosity of their surroundings, at galas and receptions.

Wren does not recognise these places. Her early memories are not of these front-of-house atria, photograph-lined, carpeted and warm, but of endless backstage corridors, unfinished and uniform in their peeling greyness, damp and poorly lit. They are memories of falling asleep on piles of coats in warm cloakrooms to the sound of applause that sounded like the lapping of waves on a beach and that seemed to go on for ever, memories of the labyrinthine corridors of theatres, operas houses and concert halls, cities within cities, in which she spent so much of the first two decades of her life. She had grown up fascinated by the hidden workings of the theatre, by the creation of impermanent spaces, by the secret mechanisms that allowed palaces to become forests, by the pulleys and weights that gave actors flight. During her mother's long hours of rehearsal, she made homes of the abandoned scenery for *Tantalus* and *La bohème* until she was retrieved from backstage by whichever unfortunate Cleo sent out to find her.

Cleo is noticeably younger in these photographs. That is to be expected, though her mother's smiles are different to those she wears now. They are less composed and there is something in the way her eyes shine out of these photographs that makes Wren feel as though her arrival was an intrusion, an imposition for which she has never truly been forgiven.

There is a framed photograph of Cleo arm in arm with Georg Solti. Before Wren hangs this photograph, she unfastens the back of the frame and removes a second, hidden photograph of Cleo with her arm draped over the shoulder of another man. The face of the man is that of an actor in a black and white film and he looks out of time in the Technicolor photograph. He is a young James Stewart or Humphrey Bogart, all jaw and muscular neck, his eyebrows arched. His head is twisted slightly away from the camera. His mouth is turned down slightly at the edges and his ears are too small for his face, like her own. She tries to picture him as he might look now, to put him into one of the places they passed on the journey between the docks and the house. Wren takes this photograph to her room, to the bag of clothes she has not yet unpacked.

On the back of this photograph there is a scrawl, a short message in what she has always presumed is O'chian and a heart, written in the same pen. None of the words is legible. She has committed this scrawled note to memory and could reproduce it exactly. There is not much to go on. The only letter she can make out is the first, which could be an R or it could be a D, and within that letter a series of loops, one of which she thinks may be an N or a V. Rodin, Radav, Dami, Donil, Dovri. She has a list of thirty or so names she has tried out for a good fit though it has got her no closer to an answer.

Though she had asked about her father countless times before, Wren became interested in him in a more serious way around the time she received Ariadne. She asked Cleo about him endlessly, though Cleo treated her questions as though they were entirely unreasonable. She could not even get her mother to part with a name, though she asked, begged, pleaded and pestered her endlessly about it. He was, though, a subject on which she would only rarely be drawn and only then in moments of weakness.

I barely remember him, she remembers Cleo saying once, after she wore her mother down or perhaps when her hangover was so severe she had no defences left. I didn't even know I was pregnant with you until after I'd left.

After this, Cleo became silent and stayed that way for hours, as though Wren had pried from her something she had intended to take with her to the grave. Cleo does not believe in explanations. Not about fathers, nor about family, nor does she believe in the reasoning behind her decisions. Wren treated even this tiny piece of information as sacred though. Had her father known about her, she thought, he would have found a way to contact them. He would have left her clues to his existence, clues that would eventually lead her to him.

For a period of a few months, whenever Cleo was away from the house, Wren searched for traces of her father in the dresser drawers in her mother's room and deep in the filing boxes that follow them from city to city. She intercepted any post that arrived handwritten. She collected numbers, addresses and names she did not recognise and within this mass of information she hoped she would find clues to her father's identity and his whereabouts. As she did not dare to use the phone in the house, she dialled the numbers she found from public phone boxes while queues grew behind her in the street. She listened for something familiar in the voices of those who answered and replaced the receiver without saying anything.

She often took Ariadne from the place where she had hidden her, away from the risk of Cleo's purges, and talked to her in the way she imagined she might have talked to a sister. These one-sided conversations often ended in Wren becoming frustrated. It felt to her as though Ariadne knew the whole story but was not telling, as if she knew something Wren could not know.

Wren has been in O for less than twenty-four hours. She has promised herself that she will leave Cleo at the first opportunity. The first opportunity, yes. She has thought about leaving before. She has certainly threatened to leave before, though each time Cleo wailed and apologised for being a terrible mother. She promised that things would be different if Wren agreed not to leave, that she would change, that they would be the best of friends again.

I cannot manage without you, she said.

And Wren, for pity, for lack of courage or certainty or some other quality, believed her. Cleo cried and Wren parented her. She has been doing this for most of her life, soothing and settling, picking her mother up when she fell down drunk at the door, holding her hair back as she vomited, tidying and cleaning around her as she slept. Well, no more.

She opens the bag on her bed and adds to the clothes, Ariadne, her passport, the photograph of Cleo and her father and the money from the wooden box. The box is stuffed with notes. Cleo does not like to discuss money, so this was always going to be a gamble but, again, her agent has come up with the goods. She has no idea how much the bundle of notes represents and she takes it all. However much there is, she is certainly owed more.

She writes a note explaining to her mother that there are things she needs to do, that in her absence Cleo will be fine. In the note, she apologises for taking the money and says she hopes her mother will understand. Once she has done what she needs to do, she will be in touch, she writes.

Before she leaves, she walks through the house and touches each of the pieces of furniture in turn. She has been doing this since she was young, when she would slip from her bed and move quietly through the rooms of the house or apartment in which she and her mother lived at the time and she would list the things she knew. The name of the city, the street, the building number, the address of the auditorium in which her mother was performing. She would run her palms, her fingers, the backs of her hands over the furniture in the darkened rooms and, as she did, she would note the texture of each piece and the extent to which it gave her comfort. She could only sleep once she had reassured herself that all the rooms still existed and that she had not slipped through the gap between this place and some other.

She places her keys on the floor in the hallway and, after a moment's thought, picks them up again. She places the keys into one of the zipped pockets in her bag. She pulls the door closed behind her and it hisses across the thick white carpet. A few thin clouds are chasing across the sky, and as they recede into the interior, the sun gradually floods the streets with the light for which O is so renowned.

She will start again. It has to be like this. Despite the bag, she takes the stairs at a skip.

PART II

The Book of Maps

FOUR

THE CITY WILL lead the way. She will be reborn to it. O has welcomed her. It has given her a sign of its intention. And as it reveals itself, she will reward it by knowing it in the way a lover knows the constellations of freckles on their beloved's forearm or their back. She will know it intimately and without prejudice.

Beyond the park, across the river, the grass gives way to scrubland and in the other direction there are more houses, though these are smaller, less substantial, a mixture of industrial units and low-rise flats, and beyond lies them the denser mass of the city.

She does not get far before her resolve begins to falter. She has thought of this moment many times but she has never thought it through, she realises, not beyond this point. She stops at a café not far from the house and orders a slice of cake and a can of Coke at the counter, pointing at the items she wants in the glass cabinet. She does not particularly want the Coke, but she feels in need of the familiarity it will provide. She takes a seat at one of the many empty tables which stand on gravelly concrete on the opposite side of the road to the cafe. The cake and drink are brought out to her a few minutes later. The other customers already seem to have been served and there is no one else waiting at the bar so the delay is, she thinks, a matter of form rather than for any more practical reason. The Coke is warm and there is no ice. Beneath its glazed surface, the cake seems to consist mostly of nuts in honey.

She becomes aware of the familiar heft of the pager her pocket as it buzzes. When it buzzes again she takes it out and covers it with her hand on the table in front of her. This is a test of her resolve. It will be Cleo with some request as to how things should be arranged in the house. She will have been thinking about it. If Wren looks now, she will be drawn back to the house. After all, she is barely ten minutes' walk from Gylincourtstriste. It would be the easiest thing to abandon her plan now. She looks around. There are no other customers at the outside tables and though there are a few people walking by the river, eyes low, fast-paced, none of them pays her any attention. There are chairs outside the doors of the apartment blocks next to the café, but they are empty. As far as she can tell, she is unobserved. Covering the screen with a finger and holding it close to her side, she stands and approaches the riverbank. She kneels and holds the pager between her thumb and forefinger and throws it across the river in the way she might skim a stone. The pager skips twice on the surface and disappears into the dark water. No half measures.

She returns to the table and takes a note from her pocket, five hundred sypari. She has no idea whether this is too much or too little, but she likes the idea that someone in the café might be about to get a decent tip, so she tucks it under the glass and leaves. Later, she will realise she has left the equivalent of roughly fifty pence for the drink and cake and a tip and by then it will be too late.

The further into the city she walks the less she can fit O to the model of the other cities she knows. Everything seems pitched together, the architecture a mix of gothic, brutalist and nondescript, the solid and the hurriedly built, buildings that seem unsure if they are residential or industrial, parks that are out of place with the surrounding houses, factories and warehouses that create dead ends in broad streets. In places, the remains of tramlines cross roads at odd angles and disappear beneath grass verges and covered walkways that run between buildings and sometimes beneath them. She avoids these, much as she avoided the subways in Paris and London.

As she walks clouds gather again and as it begins to rain she takes shelter in the remains of a tram shelter that has been left to fall apart. It must be impossible to travel anywhere quickly here, she thinks. It is a wonder that anything ever gets done. The looping streets and countless bridges seem designed to confuse. There are posters pasted to the inside of the shelter including one that advertises Cleo's run of concerts. From another, a pair of eyes stares out, bordered above and below with a slogan. DIS VIALA SEIN.

She is wondering what this slogan might mean when a man who looks like her father walks past. Not her father as he would look now, but as he appears in the photograph in her bag, her father as a much younger man. She watches him pass and then follows him at a distance as he turns off the riverside into the maze of streets. The man walks quickly, with purpose. His shoes are highly polished and though he walks along the same dirty street as everyone else, his leather soles seem immaculate.

The streets through which they walk now are ones she has not seen before and though Wren knows beyond doubt that he is not her father, he seems to her a sign she can follow, a clue, though clue is not the right word. She looks around as she walks and the city spins and she stares at the shining shoes of the retreating man and increases her pace to keep up with him. The way he moves speaks of intimacy with this place, of the kind she wants for herself. He ducks into a bakery, a stationer's, a florist's, and emerges with bags, and she waits outside for him on the opposite side of the street, taking in the buildings around her, the alleyways she would have walked past only minutes before without a thought. As he continues, his arms become full. The shapes of bread, flowers, small boxes, suggest themselves through the bags he carries. He is preparing for something. An anniversary perhaps.

Eventually, he turns off the pavement into an office block. Wren waits a moment and follows him through the door and into the lobby area where she almost walks straight into him.

He has been waiting for her. He looks confused, exasperated rather than angry, and she can think of nothing to say in response when speaks to her in *O'chian*, a stream of words she cannot understand. Now that she looks at him face-on, he does not look so much like her father in the photograph. And it is not as though she can explain to this man why she has been following him, to explain that he is, if anything, a useful sign, a temporary guide whose use has come to an end sooner than she had hoped, even if she had the words for it. Instead, she opts for a grin which he does not return. He backs away from her with his bags and boxes until he is close to the lift.

She watches the doors close in front of him and as the needle above the doors rises and, as she leaves the building, she has a sense of vertiginous abandonment. She looks around at the cinema and its attendant coffee shop, the flower and fruit stalls, the jeweller's and the restaurants. This will be her starting point, the moment of her true arrival. The crowds on the street are thinning now. The realisation that she will now not be able to retrace her steps now terrifies and excites her. The area in which she has found herself is more far built-up than the one in which her mother's house stands. The roads are narrower, busier.

A little further on, a woman stops her in the street. She is animated, insistent.

Curfew? Wren says and when she mimes a roof the woman nods. Hotel? I need to find a hotel.

The woman understands this and points, and embarks on a long explanation of which Wren can make no sense.

Thank you, Wren says, hoping to bring the conversation to an end and when it does not, she takes the woman's hands, holds them between her own and looks earnestly into her eyes.

I will be fine, she says. Honestly.

She walks in the direction the woman indicates and after a minute or so comes to a side street on her right, down which she can see a small, lit sign hanging outside one of the buildings and which reads Hotel. The otherwise nameless hotel is a narrow building between a hardware shop and what she guesses is a beauty parlour. It is not the sort of place she would choose, but it will do. At the desk, she holds up a finger and mimes sleeping. The woman behind the desk tries unsuccessfully to talk to her and, when this fails, she writes a figure on a slip of paper and passes it across the desk. Wren count out the notes from the roll she took from Cleo and tries to work out how much she being charged. The woman hands her a key on a heavy, metal key fob and points her up the stairs.

Ven-dijenia, she says and holds up fingers on both hands.

Room thirty-four is at the top of three flights of stairs that are so narrow she has to breathe in to take up as little space as possible. The room itself is large enough for the single bed beneath the sloping ceiling, a small desk and chair, and little else. The bathroom, it turns out, is on the landing below. She ought to have checked that first. The idea of sharing a bathroom with strangers is almost too much to bear, though she has paid now and it is getting late. It will do for a night. The room is warm and stuffy and the space is suffused with the smell of sweat, the evidence of previous guests or of the bodies that occupy the rooms to either side of hers. She opens the window and looks out across the rooftops. Twenty minutes or so after she arrives, bells sound in rippling peals that wash across the city, and shortly after that the light in her room goes out. She is hungry. For a while, there is little noise from outside, though, eventually, she hears the familiar scrabbling of animals in the alley below and it calms her a little. She sleeps with the window open, with her passport, Cleo's money and Ariadne beneath her pillow.

FIVE

W HEN SHE WAKES, it takes her a while to orientate
herself and to recall the events of the previous day.
The area in which she finds herself reminds her of the
red-light districts of other cities. Street traders gather on the
pavements and conduct arguments and conversations, share
food, trade items they pull from large shoulder bags, hustle
and plead. When she leaves the hotel, she does not wear the
necklace with the tumbling diamond pendant, nor the earrings with which she arrived. She hides them in a sock in the
bottom of her bag, though later she will keep them with her,
hidden in her pockets, along with her passport and money.
This will prompt a discussion in the café at which some of
us gather about the safest place to hide possessions, though
none of us will reveal his actual hiding place of choice. Some
us feel it is better, on the whole, to own nothing of value, as
that is the greatest deterrent to robbery, though who among us
does not have family silver hidden beneath loose floorboards
or behind false walls in cupboards? Someone tells the story
of a great aunt who hid her jewellery at the back of the stove
when they fled the house and when her husband, who was
the first to return, set the stove going to warm the room he
accidentally melted the lot.

As she leaves the hotel, she feels again the thrill of being in
a place she does not recognise. She has no sense of where she is
in relation to where she was the day before. She cannot return

easily to Cleo. Even so, she edges away from the hotel slowly. She will need to be able to return so she dares not go too far. She has yet to see any street signs. They are conspicuous by their absence. Aside from hotels, most of the shops here go without signs too, relying instead on their decorated shop front windows and small plaques by the door.

She stops at the first kiosk she passes and tries to buy a map.

Like this, she says to the woman behind the counter. She sketches a rough street plan of the place they are and passes it over.

The woman in the kiosk covers Wren's sketch with one hand and points out along the street with the other, back the way from which she came. She seems uncomfortable, unwilling to help.

Not directions, Wren says. I don't need directions. I need a map.

She is impatient now.

Like this, she repeats.

The woman shakes her head again and looks at her slant-ways. She is agitated, uncomfortable, as if she understands the question perfectly well but wishes Wren had not asked it.

Okay, she says. Cigarettes?

The woman understands this and after she has reeled through a list of brand names Wren doesn't not recognise, the woman pulls a packet from the shelf and pushes them over to her, a soft pack with Vaniks written on the front in gothic script. Wren buys a limp sandwich in cellophane and a lighter to go with them.

She has the sensation that she is being watched again and looks round. She is used to being watched. She has been ignoring the unwanted attentions of men across Europe since about the time she turned twelve. O is no different. Cars, mopeds and even trams slow down as they pass her. Sometimes, they keep pace with her for a few moments and the men – it is always men – speak to her through their open windows or across their handlebars. Though she cannot understand the words, it is not too hard to guess their meaning. She looks ahead or down at the pavement until they give up or until they drop back and cat-call her from a distance, provocations that turn to insults the further she gets from them. None of these requires translation either.

In her first two days, she does not dare go too far and she begins to wonder about the wisdom of having jumped so definitively with so little idea of what her next step will be. *O'chian* seems impenetrable. She has forgotten more languages than those she can still speak and she still dreams in a bastardised combination of all of them but she can find no link here to the languages either Romantic or Teutonic she already speaks and that in itself scares her a little. Her main fear, though, is of becoming a deeper kind of lost. She worries that when she goes out she will not find her way back to the hotel at all, or that if she does manage to find the block in which the hotel nestles, she will find the hotel itself gone or replaced. The last of these fears is the most irrational, she knows this, but it is the one that keeps her from walking further than the same few streets, the fear that sends her scurrying back to her room.

On her third day in the hotel, after a breakfast of bread and cold, unidentified sliced meats in the windowless breakfast room, Wren approaches the reception desk. The woman stares at her somewhat aggressively, as though she anticipates a complaint about the breakfast.

Do you have a map? Wren says. I'm looking for the aspyatsiren.

The receptionist inclines her head. Perhaps Wren has said it incorrectly.

Aspyatsiren, she says again and the receptionist's face seems to harden a little. Perhaps, she thinks, she is mispronouncing it and she is not saying the word for library at all but the word for bitch, or penis. The thought of this makes her smile, which does not help things with the receptionist. Eventually, she takes a scrap of paper from the pile on the reception desk and writes the word down as she remembers it from her guidebook.

Ah, the woman says. Aspyatsiren!

She then launches into a long description of what Wren assumes is the route to the library.

Will you draw me a map? she asks and pushes the paper and pen towards the woman.

Enna, enna, the woman says and shakes her head. She repeats her instructions, only this time she includes a series of hand gestures which Wren repeats back to her. Eventually, she is confident she will be able to locate the library, though a map would be easier all round, she thinks. She has a headache and is beginning to feel wobbly about the whole endeavour.

In the end, she finds the library more by accident than by the receptionist's gesticulated instructions. It is hidden in one of the wider, quieter roads minutes from where she is staying. Just after she leaves the hotel, it begins to rain again and after looking for the library for half an hour, becoming gradually more soaked, she takes shelter beneath a deep overhanging porch before noticing long, crammed shelves inside. She expects to be challenged when she walks in, though at first there seems to be no one else in the building. She walks between the stacks and wonders where she might find maps of the city.

Wren is a connoisseur of libraries. They are her first port of call in any new city, a kind of anchor to which she can cling. It is possible to find comfort in a library where there is none to be found elsewhere and there are libraries in every city in which she has lived. The sheer volume of books alone, their solidity and weight, is often enough to comfort her. This library has the quality of appearing much larger on the inside than the outside suggests. While there is only one door, the library stretches the breadth of several houses and, instead of a second floor, there is a mezzanine with further stacks and the roof is, in part, glass. After a few minutes there, she begins to feel the quiet presence of the librarians, though she does not want to disturb the peace of the library by calling out. She pulls books from the shelves at random. They are all in *O'chian*, dense with text, and none of the volumes she opens contains maps. It could take her weeks to find one at this rate, she thinks.

About half the space is given over to desks, which are arranged in a complex pattern of off-centre semicircles around a central mosaic on the floor. She walks over to inspect the mosaic more carefully and she is thinking that she might like to stay in this place, with the diffused light falling on her from the glass ceiling, for ever, when she becomes aware that she is not alone.

There is a young man sitting at one of the desks, or rather, he is asleep at one. His head rests on the desktop, his eyes are closed. One of his outstretched hands rests on a camera case beside him. He looks vulnerable in sleep, his neck exposed to the light that falls through the glass ceiling, and Wren watches him for a while before sitting at one of the desks, taking off her still-dripping jacket and opening her notebook. He looks about the same age as her, maybe a little older. She begins to feel warmer again in the faint heat of the falling light and she watches the young man sleeping for a while longer. She is still watching him when he wakes. He stretches and pats the camera case as if to check that it is still there and has not gone wandering while he slept. The movement seems to Wren more an instinct than anything conscious. It takes the young man a moment to realise there is someone watching him. Wren feels a sudden and overwhelming need to speak.

I arrived here almost week ago now, she says in English. It feels strange to break the silence and to talk to him in a language he may not understand but she feels it is important to do this, to talk to someone else even if they will not understand what she is saying.

It feels like I've been here longer than that, she continues. My mother is a pianist – she is in O, too, though we are no longer together.

For a moment, the young man has the look of a fox caught in headlamps, unsure what to make of the blinding light, whether he ought to run or stay put, a look that is replaced by one of confusion. He says something to her in *O'chian* and when she does not reply, he gathers his camera bag, gets to his feet and moves to the door. At the entrance, he stops and looks back at her.

It is nice to meet you. He mumbles the words quickly in heavily accented English, though she hears him clearly enough from where she is sitting. And then he is gone. Wren almost knocks the chair over backwards as she jumps up and runs to the door.

Wait, she shouts and runs out into the street after him, though by the time she is down the stairs he is already out of sight. Her coat is still in the library too. She cannot afford to lose it. Nor can she afford to become more lost herself, she thinks.

Back at the hotel, she is shocked by the sense of loneliness that settles on her and by her desire to see the young man again. Perhaps it was the surprise of him talking to her in English. She had thought that O was a closed shop. Perhaps it is not strange at all. Surely, she thinks, it is entirely normal that she would want to seek out company in a city she does not know. The feeling is enough to send her back there the next day, though she tells herself she is returning to the library purely to continue her research, searching the stacks for evidence of her father. She returns the next day and the day after. Each day her routine is much the same. She starts at the end of a row and works her way down towards the desks. Occasionally, if she finds a book that looks promising, she takes it down and leafs through for maps or illustrations. She would like to say she is methodical but her concentration is split between looking through the books and watching the door.

Few people use the library. The majority of readers are elderly men and women who nod at her when they pass in the stacks but otherwise keep themselves to themselves. The librarians seem almost to have perfected the art of remaining unseen among the stacks. When she glimpses them, they seem monkish and severe and she gets the impression they take their job more seriously than even the librarians in Berlin. She wants to talk with them but what would she say? They seem to her more like the books' gaolers than their guardians.

When she next sees the young man again, it is late in the

day. She watches him from the stacks. He sits at the same table he occupied before and while he has the same case with him on the desk, this time he has a large book of photography open in front of him and he seems engrossed.

Wren takes a seat two desks down from him and he looks up for a moment and then back down at the book again.

I've been waiting for you to return, she says.

She expects that he is going to jump up and leave again and for a few seconds he seems to be on the brink of it, though this time he stays.

You speak English? she asks.

A little, he says. I am Alexis.

He sticks his hand out and she shakes it, trying not to giggle at the formality of it.

Wren Lithgow, she says.

He tries the words out, tests them. He struggles with her surname and says it several times.

You are staying here long, Wren? he says.

I will be here for a while, she says. I don't know for how long yet.

She wants to say more but she is suddenly shy too. This is the most she has spoken to anyone since she left Berlin. They sit in silence for a few seconds and a bell rings somewhere in the depths of the library.

We must go, he says. The curfew is near.

Wren nods.

I would like to see you again, she says. Maybe you will come and find me?

Alexis says nothing. He seems torn and eventually Wren stands and walks to the door, pausing briefly at the ledger of books borrowed and returned. She looks back to see if he is still watching and, when she sees he is, she sketches, on the next empty page of the ledger, a map, just a few short lines that show the route between her hotel and the library. She marks the hotel with a star. Beneath the sketch, she writes, 14:00. Find me. and leaves it for him to find.

He will meet her. He will not. He will meet her. He will not. Perhaps he will not pick up her note. Perhaps, even if he does, he will ignore it. Right now, she is moving through O by touch, feeling her way towards answers, though with no guide, no direction. She needs a friend here.

The next day, she waits at the entrance to the hotel at two and when she sees him watching her from across the street, she waves. Alexis stays where he is and Wren walks out to meet him.

You must not make these, he says and uncurls a hand that is holding her sketched map.

Wren's face falls and Alexis says quickly, Would you like me to show you a little of my city? I can show you things that perhaps will not be on the tours that are planned.

I want you to talk to me in *O'chian*, she says.

Alexis hesitates.

You speak it?

No, not a word. I want to learn, though. I want to hear you talk about your city in your own language.

Alexis nods and starts to talk, hesitantly at first, as though he feels that perhaps he has made a mistake and she will change her mind.

Go on, she says. Keep talking.

She is not sure what he wants to impart. She listens for meaning in his inflection. She watches for it in the movement of his hands.

As they walk, she points to objects which Alexis names and she repeats the words back to him. She reads aloud the plaques on doors, words carved into clock towers and war memorials – names and professions. Alexis is patient and interested. His corrections of her pronunciations are soft, encouraging. There is a gentleness about him that she is unused to, a shy watchfulness.

They walk along the banks of the river and through an art gallery where Alexis shows her paintings she does not like but which he seems to love, paintings with discordant, clashing colours. He talks as though he believes the intensity of what he is saying will make up for the fact that she cannot understand him. Though she had not thought of him as attractive – he looks to her like a banker or an accountant, someone quite anonymous – she finds, at times during their walk, that she would like to take his hand, that she would like to get to know this shy boy much better.

The library is the last stop on the route, at the very end of the day. The library is cold now, the desks empty. Pale light illuminates the books in their tall stacks. They stand at the outer edge of the semi-circle of desks and Alexis points to the ceiling. She becomes aware of the structure of the building, the fine plasterwork of the ceiling around the central lightwell, the complexity of the mosaic that covers the floor. The mosaic depicts a firmament, crammed with stars and alchemical signs she does not recognise, and it seems to her that he is explaining their meanings or telling her a story about them. Here, Alexis gestures that he would like her to stand by the largest star in the mosaic. He faces her and puts his arms around her waist. She is not expecting this and she almost pulls away. But it feels good. It feels right. He is talking to her, his face just inches from hers.

You will like this, he says. It is a trick.

He shifts so he is standing on the star, and Wren moves with him. The effect is immediate and unexpected. Suddenly, she can hear their breathing, though it is their breathing amplified many times, as though they are breathing into a microphone and the sound is being relayed back to them on loudspeakers. She quiets her breathing and she can hear other noises too: the breathing of the otherwise silent librarians, as though they are standing just behind them and not hiding in the stacks; footsteps in the street outside; the passing of traffic; the rushing of water beneath the streets.

You're full of surprises, she says, and when she laughs, Alexis laughs too and their laughter multiplies and rains down on them and it sounds as though they are in a room full of people all of whom share their joke. And though she was not planning on doing this, she kisses him.

She kisses him and they dissolve into laughter again and she can feel the disapproval of the silent, unseen librarians amid the torrent of multiplied laughter that rains down on them and they run like children from the silent disapproval of the librarians.

I'm hungry, Wren says.

Where would you like to eat? Alexis asks.

I don't know anywhere, she says. How about that one?

She points and Alexis laughs.

You are sure?

The café is busy with couples and families talking and arguing and balletic waiters who bustle between the tables looking harassed, balancing plates and glasses and stepping over children on the floor.

Would you like me to order for you? Alexis says when the waiter hands him the menu.

Wren shakes her head, takes the menu and inspects it. She keeps the waiter waiting thirty seconds or so as she scans through the unintelligible lists of foods. She cannot tell which are the main courses and which the drinks, so she aims for one of the items in the middle.

I will have this, she says.

You are sure? Alexis says.

Sure.

Alexis shrugs and orders and the waiter bows, almost imperceptibly, and bustles away through the tables.

What do you think of our city? he asks.

It's beautiful, she replies.

You are kind, but it is not a beautiful place. Maybe it was once, he says. So, what are you doing here? You are on holiday here, perhaps?

The question floors her. She wonders how she ought to answer.

I'm looking for my father.

He lives here?

I think so.

Alexis considers this.

Perhaps we can look for him together?

I can pay you to help me, she says and immediately wishes the words back into her mouth, but Alexis laughs.

Perhaps if we make progress, you can pay for our next meal together, he says. At a modest restaurant, of course.

She agrees that she will pay for a meal at a modest restaurant.

Okay, he says. What do you know?

She tells him about the photograph and the little she knows.

I don't even know his name, she says.

Alexis nods, as though this is nothing unusual.

Maybe you will show me the photograph sometime?

When the food arrives, Alexis's is steak and chips and Wren's a bowl of thin soup in which swim scraps of a fatty, unidentified meat and out of which rises a small island of grey pap.

It is an *O'chian* delicacy, Alexis says smiling. It is a brave choice.

This is exactly what I wanted, she says and tucks in.

You like it? he says.

It's perfect, she replies. And it is not too bad, not when washed down with glasses of the wine, which has enough rough flavour to mask whatever is in the broth.

I would invite you back to my room, she says when they finish eating. But it's barely big enough for me. I am pretty sure I'm not allowed visitors either.

I would invite you back to my apartment, though it is almost curfew, Alexis says.

I'm okay with that, Wren says. Show me your apartment.

She puts her cutlery down and moves her plate to one side. Alexis pays the bill and Wren takes his hand. They catch a tram, which stops outside the building in which he lives. Alexis's apartment is on the third floor of a former industrial unit on a narrow street tucked away off one of the city's wide, looping and inconsistent arteries. As they climb the concrete internal stairs, she hopes she has not misjudged him.

Alexis's apartment consists of two rooms. The larger of the two serves as kitchen and living room. Aside from a table and two chairs, a long sofa and some bookcases, there is little else in this room, as if Alexis is attempting to maintain the aesthetic of the building's former industrial use, though Wren can see it is more that he does not know what to do with the space or does not care enough to do anything else with it than anything he has planned. The wide windows at the front overlook the street. They look out too onto the windows of the building opposite and she wonders about the lack of curtains or blinds, about being so exposed to whoever occupies that unit. Outside, there is a balcony with a low wall that runs the length of the apartment.

Alexis produces a bottle of wine and puts a record on.

His name is Domezan, he says. He is very popular here.

Alexis seems to want her approval of the music, but she just nods and continues to browse the books on his shelves.

She expects that going to bed with Alexis will be as awkward as the fumbles she has had with boys in the rehearsal rooms at Lindenoper and Auditorium della Conciliazione. Her first was an understudy for the role of Ferrando when she was fifteen and the second a young violinist whose services were not required as Cleo performed Shostakovich's Second Piano Concerto to a crowded auditorium, just after Wren had turned seventeen. In his own apartment, though, Alexis seems more relaxed, more confident.

Alexis's bed is an afterthought in the room and stands against one of the walls. The bedsheets are overlaid with drying photographic prints which Alexis scrabbles to gather and tidy when they come to bed. She picks some of them up as he tidies and makes space among the clutter. The photographs are all of people. Some of them are street shots, groups of people talking, taken at an angle that suggests the photographer was shooting from somewhere higher, perhaps from a first- or second-floor window. Others are taken through windows and again show either individuals or groups engaged in conversation or argument.

In the bathroom, balanced on shelves, there are trays in which sluice strong-smelling solutions and bottles of liquids. When she comes back into the bedroom, Alexis kisses her and, when he removes her top in one fluid movement, she has the sensation that she is a deer being skinned.

When they make love, she feels his hot breath on her neck and imagines she is joining herself to the city itself rather than to one man, as if he embodies something more than he possibly could. In bed, Alexis is intense, sure of himself, and he seems sure of her too. He whispers to her in *O'chian*. He lets her guide him and she does not know whether it is something about Alexis or whether it is being here, having abandoned herself to the city, but being with him feels like release after too long being kept in. As she comes, she holds the soaking whorl of hair at the nape of his neck and leans her forehead against his. Afterwards, as they collapse together on the bed she closes her eyes with Alexis still inside her and imagines herself full of the city's fabled light. When she reopens her eyes Alexis is staring at her with an almost fierce intensity.

They spend much of the next three days together in bed, though Wren returns to her hotel each day to pay for the room for the next night and to check that her belongings are still there. She makes a sketched map of the streets between the two buildings so she will not forget her way, though when Alexis sees this he says, This is not allowed.

You've said that before. she says. Why?

It is forbidden.

Forbidden?

The reluctance of the woman in the kiosk returns to her. Perhaps it was fear, for Wren or for herself.

O is a complex city, he says. You need to memorise the routes you use regularly.

Alexis picks the map off the tabletop, sets light to it and drops it onto the ashtray on the table.

What are you doing?

I am protecting you. This is against the law. It is for the same reason there are no road signs here. There was a time you would have been shot for possessing a map. A city with no maps and no street signs is hard to invade. It's not like that now, though the penalty is still severe. If you were found with a map now, you would be detained and possibly deported, if you were lucky.

I didn't ask for your approval, she says. Or your permission.

It is a serious offence, he says.

So, there are no maps? None at all?

There are rumours that maps of O do exist, though if they do it is a long time since anyone has made one, he says. There are stories of maps stitched into the linings of jackets. Or sewn into gloves that could be turned inside out and read, maps that were encoded into pieces of pottery or disguised within other texts, the most ingenious things. If there were any like this though, they are either well-hidden or have long since been destroyed. If you carry on doing it, sooner or later, someone will notice.

I'll be more careful, she says.

Promise me you will stop, he says. I'm serious.

She wants to laugh, but Alexis looks serious, worried even.

I will show you round, though, he says, buoyant again. We

52

will work our way slowly out from here and you will get used to it soon enough.

Alexis is as good as his word. When he is not working, he shows her the streets of Hereckl, the area in which he lives. They eat out and walk until the curfew bell rings.

As Alexis talks, she absorbs O'chian as she has every other language she has heard in every city in which she has lived. She drinks it in though it is entirely unfamiliar. It is a world away from the bastardised languages she already knows, which borrow indiscriminately from each other. It helps that Alexis speaks a little English, though he does not often use it and, anyway, she prefers to learn this way.

A week after they first meet, Alexis gives Wren a set of keys to his apartment and she gives up the hotel room. When she moves in, she is glad that Alexis is not there. He is out at work, though he has told her she should come and go as she pleases.

SIX

ALEXIS IS UNLIKE other men she has known. Aside from moments of boldness that surprise her each time, when they are alone together he is self-contained and quiet, almost shy. At first she assumes that photography is his hobby but it is his job. She finds it difficult to reconcile herself to this. He does not look like a photographer. He looks like someone more serious and sober all together. When she tells him this he says in reply that this is one of the things that allows him to do his job, that he looks anonymous and plain.

He is interested in her plan and once she has moved in he asks to see the photograph of her father. He scrutinises the scrawl on the back of the image.

It is strange to talk about her father after so long not talking about him. Whenever the few friends and later the few boyfriends she had asked about her father, she had concocted elaborate lies about him or told them that he was dead to see what effect that would have on them. What little she knew about him, she held close to her chest with a jealousy that surprised herself.

This is your mother? he says. She is very beautiful.

Do you recognise the man? she asks.

Alexis, she can see, tries not to laugh when she says this. She tells him what little she has gleaned from Cleo.

When was this taken? he says.

I'm not sure, she replies, 1979, 1978, maybe before that. It was taken before I was born. What do you make of it?

I don't know, he says. Radiet-husj, maybe. It's not a popular name, but maybe. Donats-husj, perhaps. It is difficult to make out. Either way, there must be hundreds of men here with those names.

He turns the photograph back over.

You see the grey block in the corner? This photograph was taken in one of the statue parks. There are several in the city, though I can take you to them if that will help?

It won't help, Wren knows that, though she nods and says yes, she would like to visit the sculpture parks.

You don't know anything else about him?

Wren reaches under the bed and takes Ariadne from her bag, wrapped in her silk scarf. She puts her on the bed between them.

My father gave my mother this before she left the city. Aside from the photograph, it's all I've got to go on.

She is a mechanical? Alexis says. She is beautiful. May I wind her?

She has no key, Wren says. I lost it a long time ago. I think, even if I had the key, she would not work now.

She lifts Ariadne and shakes her gently and they listen to the faint sound of loose metal parts, tumbling within.

She has travelled with me for years. She is called Ariadne.

Like in the story of the minotaur? Alexis says. She is not an Ariadne, though. She comes from here. You ought to have given her an *O'chian* name. She is part of O, you know that?

How do you know?

She is the Daughter of O, he says, as though this explains everything.

When Wren looks blank, he continues.

She is a figure from a story every child in O learns from their parents, a folk story, like 'The Complex Systems of Nikolask Syyorak' or 'Breschel and the Bear'. The story of a rich family who lost their first-born daughter. In some versions, she is the daughter of a prince of O, in others she is the daughter of a duke or one of the large trading families. In any case, she was the child of an important family. Each week, her mother took her shopping in the marketplace, to remind her that even though they were wealthy they ate the same food and walked the same streets as everyone else in the city. The girl, distracted by a toy from one of the stalls, became separated from her mother in the crowds at one of the many markets and when her mother called for her she did not answer. Her mother and father searched the market and surrounding streets. They sent out servants, and later the whole city was sent out to look for her. Her family announced a reward for anyone who could find her but no one could. Some poor families offered their daughters in exchange for the money or just for the better life the rich family could offer their children, though her family said their daughter was irreplaceable. And though there were several sightings of the girl for years afterwards, she was never found.

There are many different endings to this story. In some, she was taken by a visiting trader and smuggled out of O, never to be seen again, or sold into slavery. In the one most children are told, she remained lost in the streets for so long that she became a kind of spirit seen only in fleeting glances, out of the corner of your eye. She is always one street ahead, one turning away, and if you should chase her, you would find yourself as lost as she was. Many places have a story like this,

I am sure, a warning to children to stay close to their parents, though it is maybe resonant here as this is a city in which it is easier to lose yourself than most.

And how do you know that my Ariadne is the Daughter of O?

The girl's family was heartbroken, Alexis says. When she had been missing for several years, her parents realised that she was not going to return. They were afraid that people would forget about her and that eventually she would be lost even to their memory. They commissioned a sculptor to create a statue, so that no one would forget their daughter's face. They wanted the image to be distributed as widely as possible and, once they were happy with the model, they paid for many replicas to be made and for them to be distributed across the city. Some people say they bribed sculptors to use her face as the model for other statues they had been commissioned to make. It is still possible to find her likeness in the statue gardens, in friezes, paintings, woodcuts, in children's toys like yours. Even though her story is now twisted beyond recognition through generations of retellings, hers is the most well-known face in O. She has become a tradition. Artists, even now, will paint her into crowd scenes or as a minor character in a well-known scene, as a nod to her story. Her clothes change over time, her hairstyle too, though her face remains the same. She is a kind of emblem for the city, and she is so often seen that we barely see her at all now.

And were many of these made? These mechanicals.

I don't know about that. Her face is definitely that of the Daughter of O. She looks old, though. She looks a bit like you.

She looks nothing like me, Wren says and lifts Ariadne so their faces are level with each other.

No, not your wind-up girl, he says. Her face is too worn to show the likeness fully. I mean the carvings of the Daughter of O. The statues and paintings.

Will you show them to me?

Alexis says, yes, he will do this. Instead of wrapping Ariadne back into her silk shroud, Wren places Ariadne on a niche in the wall where she can watch over them.

Tell me more about O, she says. I want to know everything.

No one wants to know everything, Alexis says. I think if we knew everything about a place we would never want to see that place again.

Tell me anyway.

Okay, okay, he says. O is a mediaeval city. It was designed to confuse invading armies. We are not a large enough state for an army of any size, not compared to our larger, more powerful neighbours. The founders of O had enough foresight to recognise what our predicaments would be, so they designed a labyrinth city.

And the centre? Wren asks. Doesn't every labyrinth have a centre point? A goal?

That is the Kesibyr, Alexis says. The glass tower is at the centre of O. Before the Kesibyr, in the place where it stands now, there was a large, open square where dances and festivals took place, and other events we are less proud to advertise. Labyrinth or no labyrinth, we found out it did nothing to protect us from ourselves either. After our little war there was no dancing and no festivals, not for a long time after the fighting was brought under control. The new O has no need for such things either. When we announced the borders were reopening, the foundations of the Kesibyr were put in place.

And what is it? she says. The Kesibyr. What role does it play now?

It's a centre for business. It has other roles – there will be a gallery, a restaurant, and a concert hall too – but if we wish to attract banks and investors, if we want investment to come flooding in as the government has announced it will, the moneymen must have a home fit for people of their stature.

He does not sound sure of the wisdom of this at all.

They have come up with a slogan, he says. Your money is safe with us. That's why it is there, at the heart of the labyrinth city. Of course, it is a joke; there is much corruption in the city and any money that does end up here will be leached out of the centre as fast as water drains out of the Meret, but that's advertising for you.

A few days after Wren moves in, Alexis enters the apartment with a letter in his hand.

I have work, he says.

He gathers his cameras, notebooks and pens.

What work? she says.

Photography work, he says. He kisses her and then he is gone.

Late that afternoon, the electricity cuts out. After trying the lights throughout the apartment, Wren loses track of which position the switches should be in and when they come back on in the night, they flood the rooms like interrogation lamps and she wakes in a panic. Outside, there is a brief wail of police sirens, which adds to the effect that the city is constricting around her, that she has been in some way found out. As she stumbles between the rooms turning the lights off again she registers that Alexis is still not back. By mid-morning, he has still not returned and she walks to the library to calm herself.

Alexis does not display his own photographs like other photographers she has known. He does not exhibit or sell his work. He wants, he says, to be anonymous.

What sort of photographer are you? she asks him when he returns. Really?

I suppose you would say I am a freelance photographer, he says.

That doesn't explain anything, she says. What does that mean?

It means they do not need to pay me for my holidays or for when I am sick, he says.

Not what I meant.

Okay, okay, he says. I surrender. I will tell you everything.

He selects a few images from his files and deals them in an array, like oversize playing cards. The photographs are mostly portraits, taken from a distance. Most are taken through windows into apartments and houses. Wren asks how many of these people understand they are the subject of Alexis's photographs and Alexis shrugs. In some of these, the subject of the photograph is in conversation with someone else, someone out of shot. They are caught in the act of arguing, crying, laughing, debating. In one, there is a lone figure sitting at a table. There is no plate or glass or book in front of the man at the table but he is focused on something, the pattern on the tablecloth perhaps or a memory. The thread that seems to connect the photographs is the vulnerability they expose in their subjects. They are uncomfortable and raw, couples caught in the act of eating or arguing, people engrossed in their own worlds and with no concept that they are watched.

Is that not just voyeurism? she asks him. To observe like this without being observed? Is there not something distasteful about it?

It is work, he says. It is best not to think of morals.

She is arguing to provoke him, she knows this.

Who are they for?

I only have one client and that is the state. Most photographers here work for the state, though I think some of them hope – we are just about to enter a Year of Hope, you know? – that there will be more opportunities for us as O opens up to the world.

You're avoiding my question, she says. What do you actually do?

I take photographs of people who are of interest to my employers. He seems uncomfortable now.

So you are a spy? she says.

It is nothing so glamorous, he says. It is not at all what you think. It is administration, nothing more. When I started this job I made it a principle that I would not speculate about how the photographs would be used once they left my hands.

You don't ever question what you are doing?

He explains that he receives letters in his pigeonhole on the ground floor. Often, the letter contains a key or the location of a key, and an address from which he should shoot. Other times he receives an allowance for rent on an apartment or hotel room, or money with which to pay people to shoot from their apartments. Sometimes the letters specify a need for photographs of a particular person and include descriptions and other times the brief provides only a time and location.

61

If anyone covers the hours outside those for which he is responsible, he does not ask who that would be, and it does not concern him.

And you are successful at this? she says.

I presume so, Alexis says. I've not had any complaints.

And what do they do with these photographs? she asks. Do you never ask?

No, he says. Though it is impossible, in the long hours of waiting, through days in which I might watch a single door for nine or ten hours and during which time no one will come or go, not to consider my employers, though anything beyond the mechanical act of following the instructions contained within the briefs they send to me is off limits.

And if you watch other people, do other people watch you? she says.

Oh, I'm under no illusion that I am not watched myself, he tells her. It's something everyone in O is used to. It's hardly a routine job, I know. The hours are bad for the soul but the money is good and the work is regular.

A thought occurs to her.

Do you know anyone who might be able to help me? If so many people are watched, surely there's an archive of them? she says. It's possible that someone might recognise him?

It's possible, Alexis says eventually. Though if you do find him through official channels, it would bring attention to him and possibly to you as well. Bringing attention to yourself is a bad idea. I think you would be better making discreet enquiries of your own. I've been thinking about your Ariadne though. You should get her fixed. You would need a clockmaker, one of the old guard. They might even be able to tell you who owned her before. There can't have been many of these made. There is a clockmaker on Omniastriste. He may be able to help you.

Alexis writes down a name and address on a scrap of paper and hands it to her.

His name is Passhau, he says.

She tells him she will think about it.

The images stay with her. When she pictures Alexis at his work now, he is predatory. His photographs seem to her like an act of violence, these photographs, an act of destruction rather than one of creation.

SEVEN

LOCATING OMNIASTRISTE AND the clockmaker takes several days. She finds him, eventually, in a street of tightly packed workshops in a district she has not visited before. It is an uncared-for place. In the window there is a rough board on which stand three carriage clocks, arranged in a line, and by the door is a small plaque with the label, R. Passhau, Horologist. When she enters there are no lights on and no sign of the owner, just a thick, syncopated choral tick, the murmur of hundreds of mechanisms in motion. The shop is a confusion of clocks of all types and she walks towards the glass counter into the gloom beneath pendula that hang from the ceiling. Along the back wall, there is a cabinet that contains a small collection of mechanicals: a soldier standing to attention, a flock of tiny metallic birds in an intricate cage, a monk, his head bowed in prayer, an egg encrusted with garish jewels that she assumes are paste. She has been looking around the shop for maybe a minute when she hears a sound that does not fit with the ticks and creaks of the clocks and she turns to see a man in his late sixties watching her from a partially open door.

I'm closed, he says. Let yourself out. Come back again. Or don't. But let yourself out.

I have something I would like you to take a look at.

Wren wonders if she has made a mistake in her still-faltering O'chian.

You are Passhau, though?

If you are collecting taxes, no. In any case, I'm closed, Passhau says. And busy. Make an appointment and come back. Or don't.

Wren reaches into her bag and takes out Ariadne. She unwinds the scarf onto the desk.

I would like to find the person who owned this, she says.

He waves a hand dismissively.

A toy? You're in the wrong place. Let yourself out.

Passhau pushes the inner door and turns back towards the workshop.

I only want to find the person who owned her, she says.

You can take your toy, he says. He rushes back towards the counter and as he lifts the doll she is sure he does it with the intention of throwing it at her, though something causes him to stop. He places Ariadne on her wheel on the countertop, carefully, slowly, and lowers himself until his head is level with the countertop. With a finger supporting Ariadne's neck, he lowers her to the glass and with care he lifts her coat tails and looks at the workings on the underside.

Passhau says nothing for a while but continues to disrobe Ariadne on the counter, turning her this way and that, gently and with great care, as though she might fall apart beneath his fingers.

You look like you are from here but you are not from here, Passhau says, all the while staring at the robed girl. But she is. You found her perhaps? You stole her?

She belonged to my father. I am hoping you will help me track him down.

She wants to tell him about how she came to have the wind-up girl, but Passhau's attention seems to be less on what she is telling him and more on Ariadne.

What matters is that she is here now, he says.

What do you mean? she says.

I mean that she is damaged but that she is in the right place now.

He says this in the way a doctor might talk to the parents of a child who has been kept away from hospital after a terrible accident. He does not take his eyes from Ariadne, as though he expects that at any moment she might rise up from her supine position and move of her own accord. He retreats through a door in the back wall and when he returns he is carrying a small bundle of tools, a magnifying glass and a smaller lens, which he fixes to his glasses, and bends over the girl again.

If you cannot help me, Wren says. I will take her away.

I didn't say I can't help, Passhau says. Leave her with me.

And you will find out about her last owner?

I will find out what I can about her. He waves her away without looking up. I don't need to take a name. I will remember you. I will do what I can do. You can go now.

Wren pauses at the door, unsure about leaving her with him, though he will still be here when she returns, she can tell that without asking. Passhau seems part of this place, as though the shop is just an extension of him.

As Wren leaves, Passhau is still staring at Ariadne through the magnifying lens, entranced, and it is all she can do not to run in and take her back. She wonders if this is the last time she will see her wind-up girl. If Ariadne is of value, Passhau might sell her on. Wren has nothing more than his word that he will look after her.

Wren returns to the library most days. She reads of the founding of O, of the marshlands out of which the city rose and of

66

the engineers who hoped not only to eliminate the marsh but who sought also to tame the many branches of the Meret. She reads of the trading routes that were established from the port city, which were once the most profitable in the region. She stands alone in the centre of the reading room and listens to the sounds that concentrate in on her from the cupola. The ticking of the clock, the almost imperceptible creak of books stretching in their covers, and the sound of her own breathing. When she returns to the apartment, she tells Alexis of the things she has learnt and asks him to translate passages that make no sense to her, though, gradually, she stops relying on his grasp of English and they talk to each other only in *O'chian*. She wants to be sure that when she meets her father they will understand each other.

When she finds something that delights her – an account of the 1879 Snowdrop Revolution, or a story about a woman's life in a small walled community on the edge of the city – she seeks out the librarian who brought her the book and thanks him with more smiles and sometimes a brief hug. Alexis is right though. Her father is not in the library. This is a diversion. There are no books that relate to the period in which Cleo was here and no newspaper clippings either, as though the recent past is ignored entirely here. The librarians are unable to help her in this area.

I don't know why you bother with books, Alexis says. Sure, the library is safe, but you will not find him there. You should talk to some people, find out what they really think about O. Your *O'chian* is up to it now.

He is right, of course. She loves the library and the secretive librarians who now bring her volumes of histories, books that consist of oral accounts of life in the seventies.

67

They are eager to please with folk tales and mysteries. At first, when she opened the books they brought to her beneath the glass-panelled dome, she thought they lingered because they were expecting a tip, some *O'chian* custom of which she was unaware, though it turned out all they wanted from her was a smile.

One thing though, Alexis says. Don't ask too much about the war. It is still too close, too painful for most people. We are looking forward, not backwards now.

What would you know about it? she says. You can only have been a child yourself.

Very little, he says. I was too young to remember it and my parents never talked about it. We go to the memorial on Memorial Day and lay flowers but we never talk about it.

You mean you really know nothing about it? she asks, incredulous. Not even who was on which side?

Especially not that, he says. I had an uncle who was shot. He wasn't one of my favourite uncles and I didn't know him well. My mother herself almost died during the war, though that was because she caught pneumonia and there were no doctors. That was when she was pregnant with me. She recovered.

After this, she begins to walk out from Alexis's apartment again, slowly expanding the radius of her search. In the weeks that follow, she discovers the covered market and the train station and rediscovers the docks.

A month after she first met Alexis she finds herself on a familiar road and realises she has walked back to the place from which she started, Cleo's house. It is not, she discovers, far at all. She had not anticipated this moment and it comes as a shock. She observes the house for a while from the opposite side of the road and wonders if Cleo is still there or if she has moved on. There is no movement from within the house and the shutters are closed. She is still so angry at everything Cleo has withheld from her. She is angry at Cleo's manipulation, her anxieties and lies. She wonders what she ought to feel, being back here. She cannot bring herself to knock at the door. She is not ready to see Cleo. If she returns to her mother, it will be on her own terms.

EIGHT

THERE ARE SPILLAGES of light into the apartment, small floods of brightness in which Wren basks. Floor-to-ceiling windows stretch the length of the living space. They are ill-fitting in their metal frames and the room is always cold. When she is in the apartment, she often wears a quilted kimono left by one of Alexis's previous girlfriends. In the long mornings and afternoons she stands by the windows, feels the light on her skin as it streams in and tries to absorb what heat it contains. Once she has bathed in this light, the guidebook's descriptions seem inadequate, though she can come up with no better words to describe the sensation. In this part of the city at least, even after sundown, cafés spill light onto the pavement and the streets are well lit until the last tram of the evening has passed and the curfew kicks in, an immutable balancing force that ushers in a kind of profound darkness.

When she wakes in the night and Alexis is still not there, it occurs to her that he may be with another woman and if he was she would know nothing of it. When Alexis returns, though, he is attentive and kind and she pushes these thoughts to the back of her head.

Wren can pinpoint precisely the moment she realises she is in love with Alexis. It is the moment he tells her he has gained entrance to the archives of one of the city papers under some flimsy pretext, in order to look through editions of the paper around the time her mother was in the city, to see if he could find mention of Cleo or Wren's father.

I may have found him, he says and she feels a surge of love for him.

Tell me, she says. Tell me everything. Do you have copies of the information?

It is not possible to take anything out of the paper's archives, nor to make copies of things there. And I am not entirely certain.

But you think it's him?

I have a good memory for faces, Alexis says. It goes with the job. I found him in a photograph of a protest, so it is likely he was a radical, an agitator. He does not look like police. His name did not appear in the article, but there was a note of the known protestors on the photograph. His name is Illían Donietz-husj, so he is Illían, the son of Doniet.

And?

And that is all. He is a name in a photographic archive.

There must be more than that, though, Wren says.

Alexis nods. Yes, if he was a radical, there will most likely be a file on him. I do not have access to those sorts of files, though, and you will not be able to access them either. And now you have a name, perhaps it will make finding him a little easier.

Alexis tells her she might try the city directory, which lives in the library. There are three pages of Donietz-husjs and she painstakingly copies out the addresses. She has committed the photograph to memory, pictured her father older, with a beard, without hair, with scars, wrinkles. She would know his face anywhere, she thinks.

What will you do? Alexis asks.

I am not sure yet, she says, though she has already started to formulate a plan.

On November fourth, Alexis takes her to a parade. The streets are criss-crossed by bunting and the police wear their cleanest uniforms and polish their shoes and the tack of their horses. Alexis and Wren wait with the crowds, contained behind low metal fencing for the tanks, anti-aircraft guns, for colourful missiles that lie prone on flatbeds, for brass bands and banners.

Alexis puts his arm around her shoulder.

I wouldn't have had you down as a nationalist, she says as Alexis smiles up at the passing gunners and uniformed troops.

We are all nationalists, he says. It is required. Can you not feel it stirring you?

She laughs, uncertain if he is being serious or not.

Next year, they are planning a different sort of parade, he says. It will be different to this one. It will be based on the old traditions, or at least an approximation of them.

But Wren is not listening to him. She is watching the soldiers in their fatigues, assault rifles over their shoulders.

There will be huge marionettes, paper models in which there will be lights, he says.

The display of power, of the weapons of war, does not seem to concern Alexis. The parade seems to continue for hours, the weapons of the state disproportionate to its stature.

We should leave, she says. I don't want to see this.

Alexis tightens his grip on her arm, just slightly.

No, we should stay, he says. It is important that we should do that.

It is ugly, she says.

It is our history, he says. It is your history too.

72

It's the history of the world, she says. It follows me everywhere. In Berlin, the war hovers over the place almost sixty years after it finished, like some huge cloud of shame tethered to the country. We should let it go. They should put these machines in a museum and leave them there to rot. There they will become uglier each year and everyone will be able to see them for what they are.

War is still close to us, Alexis says. Our parents remember it even if we don't.

I'm going, Wren says. Let go of my arm.

You are here now and it's important you stay to the end, he says, his voice low in her ear, insistent, and Wren pulls away. She makes her way through the crowds to quieter streets and Alexis does not follow her. It is the first time they have argued and when he returns to the apartment neither of them mentions it.

If Alexis is jumpy about war, he is jumpier about the curfew, though the times immediately before the curfew bells ring in the evening and those directly after they ring in the morning are Wren's favourite times of day, the few minutes in which she can walk through streets that are empty and quiet. He is cross when she returns after the bells have rung and she laughs at him for being so serious all the time.

She no longer needs Alexis to name things for her and she is beginning to think in *O'chian* now, even to dream in it.

It amazes me, Alexis says, the way you soak up the language. It is as if you are not learning it at all, but that the words have been dormant within you and all you have to do is to encourage them.

I have a good reason to, she says. I want to be able to talk with my father when I meet him.

73

You still think you will? he says. You think you will find him?

Armed with the addresses, Wren begins to walk out from Alexis's apartment, methodically this time. In each new street, she finds a woman with a kind face and asks the name of the street she is in. She makes a note of the points at which one district gives way to the next. Each evening, she returns to Alexis's apartment, colder than she thought it possible to be, and cross-checks the streets she has discovered that day with her list. When she finds a match, she returns to that street and searches for a plaque with the name Donietz-husj. She invents a game that she hopes will not raise too many suspicions. Her black trouser suit, in which she had felt so conspicuous before, is perfect for this.

The first door at which she knocks is opened by an elderly woman.

I am here from O Telefon, she says. I am checking records. This is the house of Illían Donietz-hujs?

The woman nods and Wren feels the city shift around her.

Can I talk to him?

The woman nods again.

Illían, she shouts. Illían. It's the authorities. They want to see you.

There is a muffled reply and the two women wait until an inner door is opened and an elderly man in a thin dressing gown appears, dragging an oxygen canister behind him. He moves slowly and Wren feels obliged to keep up the act. She asks him about his telephone connection.

What use do I have for a telephone? he says. We've not made a call in years. You can take the line out, take the telephone. Marian, go and get this girl our telephone and she can take it now.

Now that she knows her way back to her mother's house, it nags at her. She is getting nowhere with her search and Cleo is still her best link to her father. Perhaps there are things she has overlooked. If she returns, when Cleo is likely to be asleep or out, perhaps see will see things with fresh eyes now.

Eventually, the balance tips in favour of returning to her mother's house. She decides to do so at a time her mother is least likely to be awake. Cleo has always disliked mornings. If she left her bedroom before ten-thirty, she considered it an early morning and most days, especially when she had been playing the previous evening, she emerged sometime around noon.

Wren returns to Gylincourtstriste with her keys and lets herself in without turning on the lights. Cleo stirs when she opens the bedroom door though does not wake and Wren feels a sense of involuntary relief. It is good to know that she is still here, that she has not overdosed and found herself in one of the hospitals about which they were warned.

Post is piled in the entrance hall and magazines spread out across the living room, bottles and food cartons on all the surfaces in the kitchen. Wren picks up the letters and collects the magazines. She tidies the kitchen, clears and cleans the worktops and puts the copper-bottom pans back in their cupboards. She is quiet as she does this, though her mother's medicated sleep is all but guaranteed. It is not what she had planned to do, though it is calming, moving through the house like this. She tries to work out if it is guilt that drives her to it.

She moves through each room except the one in which

her mother is asleep, returns throws to sofas, stacks magazines into neat piles, straightens the photographs in the hall. Reflexive actions, automatic and pre-programmed. When the house is tidy, she stands in front of the wall of photographs and looks for clues she has overlooked, for anything that might help and when she finds nothing she lets herself out and closes the door quietly behind her.

When she goes out now, she sees Ariadne's face everywhere. It surprises her now that she did not make the link before and she wonders if this is what has been responsible for the sense she has had of being watched. Alexis takes her to sculpture parks, including the one in which he believes the photograph of Cleo and her father was taken, and they walk between the statues, pointing out the ones that are modelled on the Daughter of O.

She sees posters on the walls of derelict buildings or in bus and tram shelters. She is able to translate the words on the posters now. DIS VIALA SEIN. WE SEE YOU. She wonders who is doing this watching and why, though when she asks Alexis he says he has not seen these posters.

There are other things in O that are familiar to her and it takes her a while to work out that she has seen these things in the guidebook Cleo dropped over the side of the ferry. The statue of Justice that is nowhere near the courts. The courts themselves, with the words TRUST THE LAW inscribed in the concrete façade above the huge carved doors. The former palace and cathedral.

She wonders about O's lack of beggars and hawkers. There are characters who make up a city: tour guides, flamboyant men and women who strut their wealth and status, who park their sports cars on busy pavements where no parking is allowed, out-of-work actors who haunt bookshops. O has all of these and it surely does have its beggars and touts, too, its fraudsters and pickpockets, though they are not evident to her. We admit to feeling a little pride that she does not see them. Despite its faults, the catch-all crackdown on vagrancy and amoral behaviour has driven many of these people underground. Not literally, of course, as O is built on marshland. To own a basement, even, is to display a particularly elevated status here. No, the tramps retreat to shopping centres that were abandoned during the conflict, to the outskirts, where there are empty factories and   industrial units where they can sleep. This is a temporary state of affairs. The city centre is like a magnet and they will succumb to its pull again sooner or later.

Over the next few days, she finds two more Donietz-husjs in Hereckl. At the first, the owner, a lady in her thirties, tells her there has never been anyone of that name at the address, and at the second, a neighbour opens a window and shouts down that the owner, Syán Donietz-husj, is dead. More names to cross off her list.

Wren returns to her mother's house several times. She tidies and cleans, organises the house, just as she has always done. She searches for traces and clues and finds nothing. She wonders if her mother notices the interventions, whether or not she is aware that the house is tidier when she wakes than it was when she went to bed, or if she accepts that if she leaves it for long enough that it will tidy itself. She misses her mother. Not the screaming fits or the days during which she refused to talk. Not the bouts of depression or the guilt trips, or the

77

emotional manipulation. But still, she misses Cleo and she begins to push the time at which she leaves a little later with each visit, until one Wednesday morning her mother descends the stairs, wrapped in her thick dressing gown.

NINE

IF YOU'RE AFTER money, you're out of luck, Cleo says.

I've not come for money, Wren replies without turning from straightening the photographs in the hallway.

I knew you wouldn't last long.

I wanted to see how you were, make sure you were okay, Wren says.

I had a panic attack last week, you know? And where were you? If you cared, you'd be here.

It sounds as if you survived, Cleo, she says.

Heartless bitch, Cleo says. She leaves the hallway and, when Wren follows, she finds her sitting at the piano.

I know his name, she says. My father's name.

How many times? You never know when to stop.

I have a right to know, she says. I deserve to know at least what you know about him.

Who was it who raised you? Cleo says. Who gave you everything you have? Who gave up everything for you?

Her mother has always done this. She constructs an argument in such a way that she is always the victim. Aside from her virtuosity at the piano, this is her great strength.

Something in Cleo clicks, the mechanism she employs when pushed, and her face hardens.

I'm leaving, Cleo says. It's not safe here. Tomorrow, maybe the day after. There's something coming. Something's building, like last time. I want you to come with me.

What do you mean, like last time?

Cleo says nothing.

I'm not going anywhere. I've met someone, Wren says.

Who is he?

He's a photographer.

A photographer? Her mother laughs. That's just a step up from dating a thief.

And I am sure all your boyfriends have been model citizens, Cleo?

She cannot remember Cleo ever having a boyfriend though. Admirers, yes, though anyone who meant more than that? Not ever.

I'll arrange tickets for you too. It's too dangerous here, Cleo says. They could close the borders again at a minute's notice. They probably will. It's a terrible shithole. It was a shithole the first time I was here and it's still a shithole now.

Dangerous how?

I don't have to explain anything to you.

Have you taken your pills, Cleo?

Her mother rises from her piano stool and lifts a hand as if she is going to hit Wren but, looking up at it as though it is something acting of its own accord, she drops it to her side again.

You understand nothing, she says. How could you even hope to understand? We need to leave. Coming here was a mistake. There are things you don't know.

I know you're overdue a handful of whatever it is you're taking, Wren says. You sound crazy, even by your standards. I'm not going anywhere. What are they? These things I don't know?

Cleo shakes her head then, without warning, reaches out

and grabs Wren's wrist. Cleo's fingers have the strength of grip of someone who has trained her hands and fingers to perform acts of unnatural dexterity. Still, as she pulls away, Wren is surprised by her mother's strength.

But you have not even performed yet, Wren says.

It is arranged, Cleo says. It is arranged and you are coming with me.

What are you going to do? Wren says. Drag me through the streets like this and hold onto me until the ferry leaves? You'll have to let go at some point and when you do I will run and I swear you will never see me again.

Wren surprises herself with the viciousness with which she says this and more surprised when Cleo releases her wrist. She can feel the nail marks.

Cleo slumps at the piano, straightens her back, flexes her hands and begins to play. Wren recognises the piece as the opening bars of Schubert's *Winterreise*, the piece with which Cleo was due to begin her run of concerts in O.

Wren turns to leave and as she does, Cleo says, in a flat, detached voice and without stopping playing, Leave your keys. The next tenants will need them.

TEN

STILL SHAKEN BY the argument with Cleo, Wren wanders without aim before returning to Alexis's apartment. She wonders if she is making a mistake by staying. She opens her notebook and scans through for signs she is making progress. Sure, she knows more about O. She knows a little of its history. Her *O'chian* improves daily, though she is aware, whenever someone tells her she talks the language well, that she has a long way to go. She knows how to navigate a small section of the city, between here and the docks, her mother's house, the library. But she is no closer to finding her father.

She wonders too if she will see Cleo again, or if now she will only read about her mother in reviews in the papers or on the radio. If Cleo has said she is leaving, she will leave. Their argument felt final, somehow. She sits at the table and tries not to think about her mother leaving, though she can picture with precision the events that will take place. Cleo will be gone before the removals team arrives, borne empress-like in the back of the car to the docks. She prefers to issue instructions through her agent, who will right now be preparing the new house, smoothing the way to wherever she is headed next.

Shortly after Wren turned twelve, she went through a phase of tearing out pages from magazines and pinning them to her bedroom walls, much as other girls she knew did in their rooms. When she returned home from school, she found the posters removed, though her mother would never admit that she had binned them. When Wren asked her why she took them down, Cleo would shout or cry, storm from the room or, if Wren pushed the matter, Cleo would threaten to throw her out onto the street. This daily posting and taking down of images continued for some six months until Wren grew tired of the running argument. It was the same with clothes and with other things she brought back to the house.

She is lost in this thought for so long that she does not notice it is getting dark. Light stretches across the gap between the buildings. Part of the apartment opposite is lit and when she looks across, she sees a man and a woman engaged in an intense conversation, which escalates rapidly into an argument. This argument is explosive, with the pair circling each other, waving their arms. Wren is so drawn to the scene, so concerned by what she is seeing, that she does not notice the cameras and lighting rigs at the far side of the room and when she does she feels foolish for not having realised that it is a film studio. She cannot pull her eyes away from the scene being acted out and it is only later that she wonders if she appears in the shot, as a blurred figure in the background.

Alex is away for several days. On the morning he returns, Wren is sitting at the table, her notes spread out in front of her, watching a young woman in loose clothes stretching in the centre of the studio opposite, going through a series of powerful, balletic movements. The building is close enough for her to observe the expression on the woman's face and to see the effort she puts into controlling her body like that. At the other end of the studio, a young man in black trousers and a black t-shirt is sweeping the studio floor with a large broom, after which he sets up and tests a lighting rig.

The studio is run by two filmmakers, a couple who, she

reckons, are in their mid-twenties. She sees them sometimes in the early morning as they arrive. They walk up the street together and kiss briefly in the doorway before they enter their place of work. They dress well. The first time she sees them, she wonders if maybe they work in advertising and it is only when she sees them appear again in the studio that she makes the connection. The man is pale and has neat dark hair cut short, and he often wears a blue suit and a light blue or white shirt. The woman too has pale skin and wears dark jackets and tops and heavy necklaces. They are striking, angular people and they seem suited to a different place entirely. Aside from the cameras and lights there is rarely anything in the way of set. Sometimes a standard lamp or sideboard that might indicate that the action is taking place in in a living room or a bedroom, but they use little else. After a few days, she realises that whatever they are filming is complex and serious. Much of what they film consists of long conversations and little in the way of action. She wants to be able to listen to these conversations.

They are brave, Alexis says. Or foolish. Only time will tell which.

Why? It's not as though they're pornographers. Are films censored?

No, censorship is no longer in force in O, Alexis tells her. Not officially, anyway, although foreign films are edited enough to ruin the story.

Alexis unpacks his camera bag onto the table. There is something Catholic about the attention to detail with which he arranges the tools before him, about the seriousness with which he cleans each of the items in turn. He stares at and

84

through the lenses and into the camera casing, trancelike, as though his mind is caught somewhere between the aperture and the F-stop. The activity takes his entire concentration, and when she watches him at this work, she can imagine him as a much older man, using the tiny brushes to ward off the dust from his lenses for another hour in the midst of an ongoing sandstorm blown in from some far-off desert that is in the process of slowly reclaiming O.

She is watching him clean his cameras at the table in the late afternoon when there is a sound like a gunshot and Alexis ducks, immediate and instinctive, before he recomposes himself. Wren walks over to the window. There is a grease-mark smear on the glass and a bird lying on the narrow balcony beneath the window. It is a large bird of a kind she does not recognise, with a hooked beak and dark green, dappled feathers.

There's a dead bird on your balcony, she says but Alexis has already turned his attention back to the deconstructed camera on the table.

She slides the balcony door open and approaches the bird, which still shows no sign of life. She crouches by it and places a hand on it with great care. The bird vibrates slightly beneath her touch. She returns inside, empties a cardboard box and places a towel inside it. On the balcony, she lifts the bird with both hands. She stretches both its wings in turn, flashing a shock of iridescent green and purple from beneath the darker green outer feathers. With her fingers beneath it, she can feel its small heart beating hard and once she has looked it over she sets it down in the box.

It's not dead, she says when she returns inside. It's just in shock. We'll need to look after it until it recovers.

Alexis is looking at one of his telephoto lenses through another lens and using a pipette and a tiny brush to remove specks of dust. He does not look up.

She likes to watch him as he processes prints. He prefers to work alone but, on the occasions when she sits in the room while he develops photographs, he seems to forget she is there. Just as Alexis is hypnotised by the creation of images, Wren is amazed by the way he works with a fisherman's patience, at the way the faces emerge at first without definition, the way the meaning of the image begins to coalesce over time, as though until that point the possibilities of what could emerge are without limit. Alexis does not like her to look at the photographs. There are files of them on his shelves but she respects his request not to go into them and contents herself with looking at the prints he leaves out to dry on the washing line above the bed. There are crowds, out of which he has picked one man or woman caught off guard, huddles of men deep in conversation, people speaking on phones. Sometimes, there are tens of photographs of the same person, sometimes alone and sometimes in company, as though Alexis is collecting all the connections that one person makes. As the faces become crisp and defined, raw and sharp on the dripping paper, she tries to repress the feelings that rise as she observes the intimacy of the photographs, the care he takes over them. She tries not to think about the subjects' vulnerability, which she fears will leach out of them in the night.

She pushes him again to tell her more about his work and he tells her that the place he is working at the moment is an apartment that is sparsely furnished. In the living room there is a sofa, a low table and a print of a poorly painted farmhouse, and a stand of trees in a field of cereal crop of the type from which the inedible pap she had ordered when they first met derived, he tells her. He sits on the arm of the sofa when he is shooting. When his eyes tire, he closes them for a few minutes and sits on the sofa, though if his superiors discovered this, there would be trouble for him. This is true. We are paid not to sleep on the job, though who among us has not, if he is honest with himself, not been guilty of closing his eyes for a few minutes at one time or another?

The apartment, he tells her, belongs to a couple. It has been requisitioned for him, in order to get a clear shot of his subject.

Do they have any choice in this? she asks.

No, but they are paid compensation for having me there, he says. It is a good deal for them.

They are sometimes in the apartment while he is working, he says. They are elderly and resentful. They avoid the living room when Alexis is there but he can hear them talking in low voices in the kitchen or the bedroom. Though it is allowed, he does not like to use their kitchen and he takes his own portable stove with him. The couple do not speak to him. They do not even acknowledge that he is there, which makes him feel as though he is a ghost to them, an uncomfortable presence they have to put up with until he leaves. The apartment smells strongly of mothballs and the sound of the couple rattling around in the other rooms and the sounds of the families in the apartments all around unnerve him. To drown out the noise, he listens to music on headphones as he shoots.

In the morning, Wren checks on the bird. She replaces its dish of water and throws in a small handful of seeds. She can feel the bird trembling through the cardboard, the quick beating

87

of its heart. Its eyes follow her though it remains still, nestled in the towel.

Wherever she is headed, Cleo will have reached her destination by now but, each time Wren thinks of her, she pictures her afloat on a sea of tranquilisers that will see her all the way to her new home. In the brief moments when the drugs wear off she will think of Wren. Perhaps. Wren is unsure. Perhaps her mother will just feel a great relief at having finally rid herself of her burden. Wren thinks about her empty house in O refilling with boxes that contain the lives of another family. She struggles with how she feels about it. It is quite not a feeling of homelessness, nor of becoming an orphan, as she would have expected, but it is unnerving, like an anchor has been weighed in the night and the boat in which she sails has drifted on the current.

Once a week, Alexis processes and bundles a selection of his photographs into a large envelope along with a log of image references, times and locations. He folds and tapes the envelope along the top and the sides and leaves it, unmarked, in his pigeonhole in the entrance hall and it is collected, though he says he has never met the person who is sent to collect the images.

Have you no interest in knowing the outcome of your work, to know what action is taken? she asks him and he shakes his head.

It is better that I do not know, he says. Anyway, I suspect no one ever looks at these photographs. I suspect they are filed as part of some enormous bureaucratic exercise designed to keep tabs on various people within the city, but which in reality serves only to generate more paperwork and to fill endless ranks of filing cabinets.

In the last breaths of autumn, they climb the stairs at the back of the building to the roof. To begin with, she is amused by how many other people escape to their rooftops to breathe in the last of the light. There is another city up here, a temporary one that gathers for the setting sun before retreating again to the souterrain. It is a city-wide pastime, this ritual of reflection at the end of the day, at which time, in the face of the dying sun, O's inhabitants might let their masks slip for a moment. This is not to say it is always spectacular. The evenings when clouds cover the sun are sometimes the most special. They lack the pretension of the nuclear reds, the unlikely incandescence of those dying days for which Wren can find no words in any of the languages she speaks. Even the clouds here hold their own and stretching up towards them, in the heart of the city, they watch the Kesibyr, which rises a little further towards the sky each time they see it.

It will dwarf all the other buildings in O, eventually, when it is completed, Alexis says.

It already does, she says. I'd like to see the city from up there. Down here, it is too confusing, too dense. It will take me months to understand it.

It is not possible, Alexis says. Perhaps in other places you have lived you are allowed to go where you want, when you want. But O is different. Here, you must go to the relevant authorities and fill out a form, several forms. You must ask the right person at the right time, and even then you will receive a rejection, only now there will be a new entry against your file. You will draw attention to yourself, and that is not a good idea.

They fall into silence for a while then and watch the setting sun blaze off the glass walls of the tower.

One evening, she carries the box that contains the bird onto the rooftop. As she comes out onto the roof, she looks across to see two women and two men from the film studio on the roof of the block opposite. There is a camera set up and a small lighting rig and it seems they are making a call about whether or not to continue. Heavy clouds are rolling over the city and the low sun shines between the clouds and the water beneath and casts the actors and the technicians and the city behind them into hyperreal relief in which the edges and corners of all the buildings and monuments seem impossibly sharp, the colours and shadows accentuated. The technicians are deep in conversation with one another, looking alternately through the lens and then up at the sky. The actors stand slightly apart from them, laughing at a private joke and, when one of them sees Wren, she waves the hand in which she holds her cigarette up at the blazing clouds and one of the men blows a dramatic kiss across the divide and Wren manages a smile. She raises her own cigarette in a limp return salute. It is as if the canvas of the city has been tightened and it is now rendered as a crazed or visionary artist might paint it. The technicians begin to pack up the cameras and the actors turn back towards the door.

The clouds gather in great banks in the far distance, blot out the sun, and the light changes just a minute later. Wren tips the box gently and the bird half-hops, half-rolls out and stands on unsteady feet on the edge of the low wall that borders the roof. It blinks and turns its head to look at her. She stands next to it and stares out across the city. The bird shifts so they are facing the same direction. It occurs to her that, somewhere, this bird has a family, a home somewhere in the city. She wonders how it came to be here, dazed and unable or unwilling to fly, perhaps unsure of the direction in which it should fly. When she looks around again the bird has flown. She did not sense it leave or see it fly, but she is pleased to find that it has gone, that it has reabsorbed itself back into the city. She has a sudden and almost painful longing to be able to see the city as the bird does, to understand its streets and rivers as they are, rather than as she conceptualises them. She looks again at the Kesibyr.

ELEVEN

A S WINTER TAKES hold, on days when the building's unfathomable heating packs in, Alexis and Wren watch their breath rising in front of them even inside. They wrap themselves in blankets or hide beneath the covers and play records by Andelka Domezan, Cap Kolba, Karlos Motek, music to conjure heat in the spaces between O's freezing rivers. Music to cast warmer shades over the city. On the days when Alexis is at home, in the hours during which he sleeps through the long mornings, Wren lies with her head on his chest and pictures the other women with whom she does not want to believe he sleeps. She does not know if he suspects this and, if he does, he says nothing of it.

There are power outages and during these times of darkness she sits close to the oil burner in the kitchen and reads newspapers and magazines she buys from the kiosk – *Morning Star, O'chian, Morning O*. There are photographs of open-air dances in the parks, reports of chess tournaments, theatre reviews, though there is nothing on the fist fights and stabbings or the drinking in the street that Alexis tells her are regular occurrences, nor of the arrests of dissidents and students who make trouble for the authorities. She has seen nothing of this in the city so far.

She buys things for the apartment, small items that Alexis does not care for, items that she can use as touchstones: a small plastic tourist statue of the Kesibyr as it will look when it is completed; postcards of landmarks; holders for the candles on the windowsills.

She returns to Passhau's a long month after she handed Ariadne over. He looks as though he is expecting her.

Have you found out anything about my father? she says.

Passhau waves a hand dismissively.

I have done something far more important, he says.

The feeling that Passhau might have sold Ariadne on grips her again.

Do you still have her?

That is not the right question, he says. It is not the right question at all.

That's the question I am asking, though, she says. I want to know where she came from. I explained this. I thought you could help me with this. I was wrong. I will take her back.

She has been away from her home for a long time, he says. She is the holder of secrets and she is damaged. She has been made to look old, you know? She has been made to look that way.

What do you mean?

Leave me be, he says. She won't repair herself.

I told you, I don't have the money for a repair. I'll take her away. I've wasted your time. No, you've wasted my time.

We will talk about money later, he says. Now go.

No, she says. I will take her back.

That will be, how can I put it? It will be difficult, he says.

Passhau opens the inner door and Wren follows him up a narrow staircase into a room that is part workshop and part living quarters. The large desk that dominates the room is crowded with angled lamps and articulated magnifying glasses.

Against one wall is a metal-framed bed and a small chest on which are a stove and a sink. The one window is shut and the room has a musty, enclosed smell.

The desk is almost entirely covered in minuscule golden cogs and tools.

She is truly beautiful, far more so than when she is clothed, if you understand me. She is radiant.

Where is she?

She is here, he says and gestures towards the table. This is your Ariadne.

Passhau breathes this rather than speaks it as if he is afraid to disturb someone who is sleep.

What do you mean this is her? she says. Where is she?

This is your Ariadne.

Wren can make no sense at all of the items on the table at first. The first thing she recognises of Ariadne is her grey robe, which hangs on a pin to one side of the desk. Beneath the robe, laid out in a neat line, are the panels of her body. The rest of the surface is covered in row upon row of minuscule cogs, wheels, barrels, pinions and springs on white cotton cloths. There are far more there than she would have thought could fit in the small figure. There are papers, too, on which Passhau has drawn complex mechanisms and calculations. She feels she might breathe on these tiny workings and they would scatter. It is like looking into the stuff of life itself, as if she has stumbled on someone involved in a complex and risky surgery rather than attempting to repair a machine.

She is unlike anything that is made now, Passhau says. She is exquisite. Her mechanism is the most complex I have seen. There are dials within dials in the shape of roses and carnations. She is a garden thick with these tiny floral cogs and gears. She is spectacular. I have done almost nothing else since you brought her in. She has consumed me. I think you have no concept of just how complex the mechanism is, how subtle. She is a work of art. Not on the outside perhaps. On the outside she is quite ordinary but within she is exquisite. She will take me weeks yet, months perhaps.

Why would someone take so much trouble on the inner mechanism and not on her appearance? she asks.

There could be many reasons for this, Passhau says. We all have secrets, don't we? I am on the very edge of understanding her. So, you see, you cannot take her away.

But I cannot pay you, she says, exasperated. And you have not been able to do the job I asked you to.

That is unfortunate, Passhau says and Wren sees that he never intended to find out anything about her father, that Ariadne fascinates him and that he has now forced her hand. Unless she is to take the cogs and springs from his desk, she must wait.

When will she be ready? she asks.

You may as well ask a tree when it will be ready, Passhau says. She will be ready when she is ready. That is all I can tell you. Now, go.

Each evening, whether Alexis is there or not, Wren wraps herself in a blanket or dresses in the thick kimono and walks up to the roof to watch the sun set. When there is no sunset, she watches the haze-glow that gathers in the direction of the port, and the trams as they drift by below. It amazes her, given how regularly the trams run during the day, that grass grows between the rails, that the grass seems to be in a constant state of reclaiming the city. She watches the small brown birds that alight on the cables that run parallel to the tram tracks, the clouds of wings that lift into the air as one when trams pass and which come down to rest before the wires have stopped humming. Long after the curfew bell sounds, she watches the empty street below for foxes to poke their noses out from behind the bins in the alley she can see on the opposite side of the road. Alexis comes and goes.

In bed, she continues to think of him with other women. She gives them the faces of women she sees in the streets around the apartment. It is the turn of a tall redhead this evening. She sits astride him in a kimono robe of the type Wren has been wearing, open from the neck down, one hand on his chest and the other on the bedstead. Alexis is staring up at the woman though she does not look back at him. She stares ahead at the wall, as though the wall is not a thing at all and she is staring through it at Wren instead as she twists in the sheets, jealous and aroused.

One Monday at the beginning of February she follows him. He should not be difficult to follow. He looks off balance carrying his large camera bag and she watches him at a distance before following, but by the time she comes to the first corner she has already lost him. There are too many underpasses, bridges, turnings off the road, and he moves too quickly. He is sure of himself and his movements in a way she feels she could never be here.

I don't believe you're working on a project at all, she says to him when he returns. I've seen nothing of it. What do you actually do all day?

And your work is so important? he says. What are you doing with all this time you have?

At the beginning of December there is a rash of posters pasted to lampposts and in doorways that were not there before. These posters carry the same slogan as the ones she had seen before, WE SEE YOU, and they depict the faces of men, though does not recognise any of them and she is unsure of their significance. She has seen no other flyers, no adverts for bands or for meetings, and the posters stand out, though when she passes by the same streets even a day later she sees they are removed almost as quickly as they are posted.

She puts on more layers and starts to walk further afield, back towards the docks where she spends hours walking in the covered market among the stalls of bruised fruit, radios and women's stockings. She is captivated by the stallholders, by their faces, hard as root vegetables, by the baskets of chickens and other small animals she does not immediately recognise, by the butchers with their piles of trotters, cleaved forelegs and hogs' heads, by their aprons with sunset bloodstains. She marvels at the hidden lives of the city's restaurateurs, the chefs and grocers who move between the stalls with practised ease, professionals who weigh herbs in their hands for some hidden quality, who hold melons up to the light. On occasion, she walks into empty or almost-empty churches. Alexis tells her the city is antireligious on the whole, though she sees evidence of religious hangovers, crosses, icons in windows and niches, references to scripture scrawled on the walls. There is something comforting in its routine, its gravity, its predictability, the immovability of walls, the weight of furniture, the fact that places endure.

One of her regular trips is to Passhau's shop. She tries the door. It is still locked. One of Passhau's neighbours, who watches her from his studio and wears a stained leather apron, says he has not seen Passhau in weeks.

He has your clock? Don't worry too much, he says. Passhau takes his own time.

The man laughs at his joke and returns to his studio and Wren wonders again if she will see her wind-up girl again.

Often, she wakes in the night in the pitch darkness and casts her arm out for Alexis. When she finds him there she is surprised, and when she finds him gone she is disappointed. Sometimes, she cannot remember when he left, whether it was the previous day or while she has been asleep. There is a phone in the apartment but it never rings and in any case she has no one to call. She thinks about contacting her mother's agent to find out where she is now, but it seems too much like conceding defeat and she stops herself with her hand on the receiver.

TWELVE

O N NEW YEAR'S Eve Wren wakes before it is light. She knows, without having to check, that Alexis is not there. She registers his absence as a coldness in the bed. She wonders whose bed Alexis is waking up in, rolls out from under the covers and sweeps Alexis's shirt from the floor. She drinks coffee, showers and dresses, and stands at the long mirror to brush out her hair. She cannot shake the thought that he is with someone else, that he is not in the place he claims to be.

When he returns, Alexis is more preoccupied than usual and when he removes his coat and she takes his hands in hers they are cold.

It is a colder winter than any I remember, he says.

Where are you working? she asks.

Right now? On the edge of Erlotz, he says. I have the keys for a room which overlooks the sculpture park. It is cold. So cold the shutters jam. I would rather be here, with you.

I don't believe you, she says. Take me there.

Now?

Now. Show me.

Are you accusing me of something? he says.

I want to see it, this place you are working.

Alexis shrugs.

It is cold out.

They walk for maybe forty minutes until they reach Erlotz.

She does not recognise the park nor the area in which it is located. Alexis shows her through into the hallway of a tall building on the road opposite the park. It is all dark wood and there is a paternoster lift that screeches every few seconds and lurches as it heads to the ground floor.

I'll take the stairs, thanks, she says.

There might be someone working in here, I'll check, he says, as he unlocks the door, though she follows him through.

The apartment is as he described it. There is little furniture aside from the sofa by the window, an ancient cooker, a heavy glass ashtray which sits on the sofa. The walls had, at one time, been covered in a light brown wallpaper that is only evident in scraps where it has caught, being taken down, and the floor is, in places, either threadbare carpet or floral linoleum. It is a miserable place and the smell of cold soup catches in her throat. It is like a film set, she thinks, like something out of a documentary set in the early 80s. They ought to be wearing brown – Alexis, a brown corduroy suit, Wren, a knitted brown dress with a yellow knitted flower on the shoulder.

You are here? she says. All the time?

Mostly. I sit here, he says, perching on the sofa's edge. I sleep on the sofa. The stove works, so I make food there sometimes.

Who are you photographing?

Does it matter?

It's seedy, she says.

It's work, he replies. Are you content now that I am where I say I am? Can we go home now?

We should walk through the park on the way back, she says.

There are few people in the park and they have the statues

to themselves. Like the buildings around the park, the statues are of varying styles, from classical busts and figures from myth to modernist, abstract concrete sculptures. She can spot the statues that have Ariadne's face now and there are several here, stone angels and naked dancing girls. In some cases it is difficult to be sure as many of the sculptures are of poor quality, the faces slightly distorted, the proportions of noses and ears slightly out. Some have lost arms or heads and these lost appendages lie in the long grass beside them.

She stops at one, a statue of a military commander, slightly larger than life. It is part of a game they have played before, a game in which they take it in turns to reveal something about an object or a building to each other.

What do you think? she says. I think he looks bemused. He's unsure of what he's doing here at all. I'm not sure this is what the artist had in mind for him. I'm not sure that this is what he would have had in mind for himself. He thought he would be commanding armies for ever and now all he commands is the pigeons. Maybe the artist got it right, after all. Maybe he knew he would end up here, with all the other relics.

Alexis still has a sour look on his face, sore at being accused, though as they walk he softens.

Alexis takes her hand and leads her through the park to another statue, one that stands on its own at the edge of the park, slightly obscured beneath the overhanging branches of the trees.

This one is my favourite, he says.

Who is it?

He was a gift from Greece, Alexis replies. But that's not the point. The point is that this statue had been here for years, and one day in the early 70s, a dignitary visiting O – I forget his name – was walking here and remarked to his companion, one of the city's high-ranking administrators in the Department for Cultural Activities, that he was surprised that the statue displayed this man's penis. The administrator said yes, it was a vulgarity and something ought to be done about it. After all, children might see it, or perhaps one of his superiors, and if word got round that he had done nothing about it, he would be sacked at the very least. When he returned to his office, he ordered the penis to be knocked off the statue, and when it was, the statue became quite infamous, especially with children. Several prominent artists protested that this was unacceptable and many letters were exchanged between officials on the subject and following one of these the senior administrator for culture ordered that the penis should be reinstated. Unfortunately, the sculptor the administrator commissioned to do this couldn't find the same coloured stone, and he repaired it using stone of a much darker red stone, which made the penis stand out even more, and so attracted more visitors to the statue. There were many songs written about it, and poems too. It became the most visited statue in the park. Eventually, they moved him here where he'd be forgotten but we've never forgotten him and we still sing the songs.

She laughs and they continue on the path that follows the riverbank, her doubts suppressed.

In Madrid, she says. In Paris, in Seville, everyone would be out at this time.

The stone tynyn tables of the park are empty – no one is playing – and the low sun casts long shadows from the stone figures, the busts of politicians, artists, scientists, some of whom Alexis knows the names of and others of whom he can tell her nothing.

New Year isn't a big thing here, he says. Aside from the military parades, there are still few public gatherings.

Are they banned?

Yes, but it is not so much that, he says. It's a hangover from a history that everyone is trying to forget. In the absence of guidance, few are prepared to challenge the way things are. I am hopeful, though. The Parade of Lights will be different. Maybe this year things will be different.

Will there be restrictions at this parade? she asks.

A few, he says. But none that will bother anyone.

Like?

There are restrictions on the types of lanterns that can be created. They must be animals or creatures from stories, not people. The administration is terrified that they will be lampooned, or that people will create grotesques of anyone they want to embarrass. But the curfew is to be lifted for it, as a show to the world that we are open and free.

When they get back to his apartment, Alexis makes a phone call and announces that they are going to the theatre that evening.

It's Theseus, he says. I thought you might like it.

She can see this gesture for what it is, an olive branch. He has not intended to neglect her, he says, he is sorry. He will be more attentive from now on. She will settle for him being more present, she says.

That evening, in the depths of the stalls, she watches, entranced, as Ariadne circles Theseus who in turn circles Asterion, each character lost within his or her own labyrinth, walking tortuous paths around the others, passing without connecting. She feels Ariadne's longing for escape as if it is her own and she feels for Theseus too, walking unquestioning through the maze to confront something of which he has no understanding, and Asterion, alone and confused in the darkness, unaware that he has been hidden and is now hunted because of his parents' shame.

Afterwards, they go to Vyala's where they serve food at the bar and it is always busy. They have left it late. Afterwards, Wren refuses the taxi the barman has ordered for them. The driver is holding open the car door when they emerge from the restaurant and she ducks his outstretched umbrella. She pulls Alexis with her, and the two of them ignore the driver as he shouts after them down the road. They take shelter only when they reach the apartment block, beneath the shallow overhang above the door. His voice is a heavy whisper in her ear. She smells wine and garlic on his breath and leans against him inside the curtain of rain. Behind then, the last tram passes by and Alexis fumbles as he punches in the door code while trying to maintain the kiss.

She is still high from the performance and the wine. As they come into the harsh light of the lobby, she pulls at his sleeve and leads him up the staircase and when they pile in through the door and Alexis collapses onto the sofa, Wren straddles him and puts her face close to his. She reaches a hand up and puts a finger to his lips, which are darkened by wine.

Did you like the play? she asks. Tell me, Alexis, what did you think?

She can feel her accent as she speaks, more heavily inflected than usual. She feels as though she is on the edge of something, as though at any moment she might tip off. She can feel the shapes her lips make. Alexis looks dazed. As happy as she can remember him looking. She swings herself off him, walks towards the bedroom and sets the shower running in the adjoining bathroom. She watches him for a while from the bedroom doorway as he kneels on the floor and chooses a record. He holds the sleeve carefully and eases the disc out, touching it only on its outer edge, his entire concentration focused on the execution of this one task. She turns away and from beneath the shower a few moments later she hears music from the room next door and she feels the light skin buzz of having drunk too much. When Alexis comes into the room Wren is sitting naked on the bed, drying her hair with a towel.

She sits, throws him the towel and pulls back the bedsheets.

Would you turn the light off? he asks, his fingers at the top button of his shirt.

She shakes her head and watches him through the hair that has fallen across her eyes as Alexis undresses and climbs into bed and they listen to the music playing from the room next door.

Well? I'm still waiting, she says. She rests her hand at the top of his thigh beneath the covers and traces a circle with the tip of her finger.

She takes back her hand and rolls towards him, pulling the cover beneath her as she turns. She raises an eyebrow. Doubt has crept in unannounced. Her head swims in the darkness. She does not understand where her anger is coming from. It is the frustration of the seeming pointlessness of her search, the lack of handholds. It is more than that. It is nothing. She is behaving like her mother.

Yes, okay. I liked it, he says.

That is a bullshit answer, she says. Do you like it more than the play we saw last week? More than the last book you read? More than you like fucking me, perhaps? I do not think that you see me at all. Not really.

She rolls away again to the edge of the bed and Alexis does not follow. He turns out the bedside lamp and they listen to the repeated tick of the arm of the record player as it tries to relocate itself but neither of them gets up to do anything about it.

You know what your problem is, Alexis? You know what the problem is?

You're behaving like a child, Alexis says. And it's late.

She wonders if he is going to continue. She can feel his body begin to relax as it surrenders to sleep. She is not ready to call it a night, not ready to back down, and she pulls him back towards her and into a kiss, the ferocity of which surprises even her.

THIRTEEN

THEY WAKE THE next morning to a dark sky that does not brighten but instead rolls itself into a storm. Alexis stands at the window and Wren watches him as the clouds gather above and heavy rain begins to fall.

I have to go, he says.

You can't shoot in this, surely? she says. Nobody will be going anywhere today.

I have to go anyway.

You could stay and we could do something else instead, she says. You can keep me warm.

I'll be back soon.

By the time the sun sets, though, he has not returned. There is something wrong here, she knows it. A cold static fills the evening. It is too cold to leave the apartment and Wren drags the sheets from the bed to the sofa. Convinced she will find evidence of his other women in the neat folders of photographs Alexis has asked her not to look through, Wren begins to take prints from their folders. At first, she flicks through without much purpose, though as she takes more and more from their files, she begins to arrange them on the table. She makes a pile of the images that mean nothing and another of the women with whom she thinks Alexis might have slept. She will confront him with this when he returns. Each file is meticulously labelled. Dates, times, locations. These photographs go beyond his job, surely. They are too intimate somehow. She pulls files out at random at first, taking care with the first few, though after a while, she tips the photographs onto the floor and sifts through them there. At the kitchen counter, she makes a list of the dates she knows he has not been in the apartment and focuses her search on those. The first few reveal nothing much but opening the fifth file she finds a photograph that stops her completely. At first she does not understand. It is a mistake, surely? She is mistaken. She releases a breath she had not been aware she was holding.

It takes her a few moments to process. It looks like a posed shot. In the image, she is drinking, both hands wrapped around a large mug that partially obscures her face. She is lost in thought and looking out of the window of the apartment though not in the direction of the photographer. The shot is taken from somewhere outside, from one of the apartments opposite or possibly from its roof. She feels a wave of nausea pass through her. She chokes. In the same file there are several other photographs of her in the apartment, taken from somewhere outside, of her crouching in the street, making notes, or walking, lost in thought in one of the city's parks. She opens more of the files and in twenty minutes she finds hundreds of images of herself, at different times, in different clothes, in different places. In some she can identify the place they were taken and in others it is unclear. The prints at the top of the pile are recent, though there are shots going back to the day of her arrival, of Cleo and her disembarking the ferry, of the two of them at the door of Cleo's house. She has been holding her breath again and the action of breathing threatens to turn to panic. She turns through the images faster and their profusion just makes things worse. She feels the room spin. She drops the photographs and puts both hands over them, though tens of pairs of her own eyes are now looking back up at her from between her spread fingers.

Fuck. She needs air. She needs a cigarette. She stands and walks up onto the roof and when she returns to the apartment she looks over the photographs again. Talking with the woman in the kiosk close to her mother's house. Walking the edge of the sculpture park. In the covered market, picking fruit and flowers. Browsing the shelves of a bookshop, passing her hands over the spines of novels written in a language she could not understand at that point. She hardly recognises herself in some of them.

A phrase from the play they watched together comes to mind, an approximation of something Asterion had whispered to Theseus in the moments before the minotaur's death.

You only see what you want to see.

She has been blind. It has never occurred to her that she might be one of Alexis's subjects, that he has been paid to pass on information about her. He has been photographing her since she arrived. To what end is he doing this?

She will confront him. But he does not return that evening and she sits at the table with the photographs laid out in front of her. She wonders if he is outside the apartment at that moment, waiting for her to walk out onto the balcony or to come close enough to the window to photograph and she moves into the bedroom and piles the photographs on the table by the bed. When she slips beneath the covers she is unable to sleep. When she finally does, the images seep into her dreams and when she wakes she is tangled in the sheets and the photographs are now all around her, on the cover and beneath it and beneath the pillow too, though as she gathers them into piles a new plan begins to cohere.

In the morning, before the bell that ends the curfew rings, she burns all the prints in which she appears and all the negatives she can find too. The negatives bubble and contort in the oil burner. They fold in on themselves and smoke and she finds she has to feed them into the fire in small batches in order for them to catch. The smell from the burning acetate is overwhelming and she covers her mouth and nose with a scarf, though it does not help at all, and instead of burning the rest of the prints she half-fills the bath and tips in the trays of chemicals from the shelves, scoops up handfuls of prints from the floor, drops them in and watches as the colours and the sharp lines on the prints bleed into one another. As the prints float and sink she recalls the boxes of camera equipment that are still in the apartment. She gathers them in the bathroom in their cases and, as she takes out each prized item and drops it into the bath, she oscillates between feelings of guilt and anger. Guilt at destroying Alexis's precious equipment and anger at his betrayal of her.

Before she leaves she erases herself from the apartment. She collects every item she brought with her and returns it to the bag, and all the things she bought since moving in. She retrieves small items of jewellery left on a bookshelf, books on the table by the sofa. By the time she has finished, the only signs she has been there at all are the burned and drowned photographs and negatives. There is not a stray hair on a pillow or a forgotten toothbrush or comb, just the smell of her ingrained into the sheets and pillows, in the fabric of the sofa.

She imagines Alexis's gradual realisation, his confusion at the lingering smell of burnt film, residue and oils in the grate of the stove that will smoke when he turns it on. He will look for signs that she will return. He will empty the bins for receipts or notes. She can picture him opening drawers in the bedroom and finding only his own clothes there, searching beneath the bed and under the mattress, lifting the rugs in the living area. She sees him picking his photographic equipment out of the bath, each piece ruined.

When Wren gets to the door, she stares at the street for a moment, takes a deep breath, pulls her bag in tight against her back, and runs like hell.

PART III

A Photograph of Wren Lithgow

FOURTEEN

I T IS THE fourteenth of February. The river runs dark
beneath the ice and the ice increases its hold on the houseboats, on the tips of willow branches that overhang the bank,
on foundations of houses and undercut factories. It squeezes
the city like eels shifting in their sleep.

Further into the city, narrow channels run down the centre
of the wider waterways and by the end of the month even these
will freeze and children will skid from one side to the other,
forming new alliances and feuds with the gangs from the opposite bank. For now, they eye each other across the thickening
ice. The inhabitants of the houseboats that line the banks of the
Meret discuss the likelihood that their hulls will crack under
the weight of the ice that has formed around them. They predict
that at a certain thickness it will break through the walls and
they will all find themselves sinking during the thaw.

The clouds of the previous few evenings are gone and it
is bitter and clear. At the port, stevedores continue to unload
containers from cold ships. They arrange them in piles that
grow and shrink and disappear entirely while they bitch and
moan about pay and about the bite in the wind that blows in
from the sea.

She will leave O. She will stay. With each step, Wren changes
her mind. She memorised the number of her mother's agent
a long time gone and it would be easy enough, though the

thought of chasing Cleo and throwing herself at her feet fills her with self-loathing. She has not achieved any of what she set out to do.

Alexis will want to find her, to explain, to reel her back in, but unless he chases her through the streets now, unless he is watching her this very moment, he will have nowhere to start. She will not return to Hereckl nor walk the routes they took together. He will ask around the neighbours. He will return to the library and stand beneath the cupola and hope to hear her in the concentration of sound but he will not find her there. She will be an absence.

There are things she needs to do. She knows the jewellery district from her explorations of O and she makes for a small shop, one of the exclusive places that display little in their windows. The shop is not open and Wren bangs until the owner comes to the door, bleary eyed.

I have something to sell.

After he has pored over it with an eye glass, the jeweller holds the pendant up by the chain and the diamond tumbles within it in its tiny box.

Fifteen thousand, he says.

It's worth ten times that.

Seventeen thousand. You have stolen this. That is clear.

I will take it elsewhere then, she says.

And everyone will tell you the same, he says. Take the money.

Forty thousand.

He laughs briefly and jiggles the pendant so the diamond tumbles again.

I should report you, he says. It's my duty to report you. Perhaps I will get a reward for it.

Thirty.

Twenty.

They agree on twenty-five and Wren takes the proffered notes and though she is ready to abandon Ariadne now if necessary, she makes her way to the clockmaker's. She pushes the door to Passhau's shop and is surprised when it opens.

The shop is exactly as she remembers it and it seems to her that not one clock is out of place. Even the syncopation of the ticks sounds exactly the same. As if no time has passed at all. This time she walks straight to the back of the room and bangs on the door and after a moment Passhau emerges. He stares at Wren and she watches emotions pass across his face like clouds.

Wait here, he says. He disappears through the inner door and closes it. She follows him through, though by the time she reaches the top of the stairs he is already returning and he ushers her back into the shop.

It is obvious that you are not from here, he says. *O'chians* are used to waiting. These things take time. Everything in time.

He has a package in his hand, which he places on the glass and unwraps gently. Ariadne is almost exactly as Wren remembers her, though her grey coat is brighter perhaps and the paint on her face fresher. She looks somehow more familiar. It is as though the long autopsy and reforming of the wind-up girl has never happened, but that she has been on a long recuperative holiday. Wren looks at Ariadne for maybe thirty seconds before she notices that Passhau's attention has turned towards her with a look of expectation.

I have spent weeks with her, months now, he says. I have worked all day and all night. No doctor has ever performed surgery as delicate or involved as I have. I have brought her back to life. A piece like this will come across my desk once in a lifetime. Everything else will seem ordinary now. There are maybe only two artists who would have been capable of creating such a mechanism. Mizhein perhaps or Roisten. I had heard rumours of pieces like this but to hold one, to restore one, it is a gift. A piece like this is only ever on loan.

Is she ready? Wren says. Can I take her?

I cannot give her back to you for nothing, Passhau says. I must eat. I must pay my rent, my taxes.

Wren takes out the money from the jeweller.

This is everything I have, she says. All of it.

For a moment, the clockmaker seems torn, but he pulls the notes over to him and pockets them without counting them. He takes out from the pocket in his shirt a small, velvet bag, which he places on the glass and pushes it across the counter.

Your Ariadne's key, he says. It may not match the original exactly, but it is the best I am capable of.

He says this with the tone of someone who is intensely proud of the skill he has demonstrated and Wren takes the tiny key from within the bag and Passhau watches as she inserts it into the slit in the folds of the grey coat.

Go on, try it. You must not be afraid of her. Wind her. Seven full turns, no more, and then set her down.

Wren lifts Ariadne from the glass, feels her familiar weight and winds the mechanism with great care. There is pressure as she turns the key, though the movement is smooth and there is no sound from within the casement. When she has completed seven turns, she removes the key and places the girl on the counter. Ariadne does not move immediately. She seems to Wren to be composing herself, considering her route. When

118

Ariadne moves, the slight angle at which she stands when she is resting disappears and she moves with a sort of mechanical confidence. She glides with no noise, the hem of her grey coat just brushing the glass surface, and the two watch in silence as she pauses, turns and continues in a different direction, glides forward a short way, pauses and turns again. She repeats this about twenty times in all and the whole movement takes perhaps a minute.

She is beautiful, Wren says when Ariadne comes to a halt. It seems an entirely inadequate thing to say given the precision of the wind-up girl's movements, the sense of life within her.

She is far more than her movements, Passhau says. It has taken me a long time to understand how she works. She is remarkable. She is capable of more than I thought possible. Now, I have to return to work. You've cost me far more than you have given me for her. Keep her safe. She is precious.

He says this quickly, as if trying to control himself and it occurs to her that Passhau might cry, such is the weight of emotion with which he looks at the wind-up girl as Wren winds her back into her cloth, places the bundle into her bag and loops the key on her necklace.

Before she leaves, Wren steps around the back of the counter and approaches Passhau. He steps back but submits to her embrace.

Take good care of her, he says.

When she leaves Passhau, Wren makes her way through the city on foot to the docks where she sees a ship depart. She pauses briefly to watch the columns of smoke that rise from the funnels in volumes that might suggest they are the cause of all the city's thick, damp air. A bow wave glides on the still water before the hull of the departing ship for a few metres before it is lost to the sea mist.

The covered market is still mostly empty when she arrives, though the stallholders have already filled the space with their noise. She likes the talk in this place, the arguments over vegetables and fish, over the quality of the day's catch. The calls and the echoes bounce back from the high glass ceilings and add to the sense of confusion. The stallholders communicate in gestures in any case, rapid hand signals delivered across the halls, a language she presumes they have developed specifically for this place.

She passes several tables of crushed ice awaiting the arrival of fish. The stallholder here stands as she approaches, as he does each time she visits the market. He gestures for her to sit in the chair he has vacated, barks an order at a boy who is shivering as he spreads more ice and turns back to her, smiles, offers sweet tea from a flask. She smiles back.

Not today, Oril, she says. Tomorrow perhaps.

The light is gelatinous and inconsistent in the market at this time in the morning. It is at least as cold in here as it is out on the docks. She walks past more rows of empty tables in the arcade adjacent to the fish hall. Meat in crates ready to be unpacked, vegetables, dried goods stacked high, silhouettes of men pulling carts. In the next hall, the flowers are out already, condensed fields of colour, deep reds, purples, yellows transplanted from their acres. As she passes, she accepts a flower from a woman who is unpacking crates, thanks her and moves through to the furthest of the halls.

As far as she has seen there are no second-hand shops in O. But beneath the stained-glass roof of the market, at its furthest reaches, there are long tables piled high with clothes, unsorted and sold by weight. Tattered shirts, ball gowns and suits in the old style with labels that announce they were cut by the city's finest tailors. There are uniforms from the war, fatigues, jack boots, as well as hats and stoles in various stages of decay, scarves in furs of mink and long-haired fox. Here it is possible to buy a coat and find within one of its pockets a letter to a lost love or a poem scribbled on the back of a till receipt or a handful of forgotten coins.

She picks from the piles a full-length coat with oversize lapels and several large pockets, and a scarf and hat. The coat has a lingering smell but she can deal with that later. It is a coat of the type she has seen many women in the city wearing. She adds a few shirts with floral patterns, dresses, long jumpers in colours and patterns that are as unlike the clothes she usually wears as she can find. The stallholder takes the clothes, bags and weighs them. Wren changes in the shadows of one of the still-dark stalls nearby, takes her old clothes back to the clothes stall, hands them to the woman and refuses the handful of change she is offered in return. Propped up by the stall is a mirror in a wooden frame with hinges still attached and, when Wren sees herself reflected in it, she almost smiles. She is not there yet though. It is not enough.

It is beautiful hair, the hairdresser in the small booth says. Too beautiful to cut. Are you sure?

Yes, I am sure.

The woman cuts her hair even closer than she asks for and Wren watches as her hair amasses, black on the white-tiled floor.

I will use your hair for a wig, the hairdresser says. There is good money in it.

When the woman holds up the mirror Wren pushes her fingers across her scalp and enjoys the sensation of the soft stubble against her fingertips. She puts the hat back on and as she walks out of the hairdresser's she feels less self-conscious still. When she sees herself reflected in a window she barely recognises herself.

As she works her way back into the city, the mist floats above the new skin of ice on the river and, as it lifts, the sun plays off the thin strip of water that runs down the middle. She imagines the river as a network of silver threads that works itself through the city. On the opposite side, in the spaces between the houseboats, there are anglers hunkered down in thick coats against the cold with long poles that reach out across the ice to the open water.

She is sure now that she looks nothing like she did when she left Alexis's. Still, she is careful not to retrace her steps. The streets are still mostly empty. Wren ignores any street she recognises, takes paths that she has not taken before, and by the time she reaches the train station, there are crowds on the concourse. On one of the station's walls, there is a huge noticeboard on which are posted lost-and-founds, items for sale, rooms to rent. This is the one stop she must make before she moves on. She stands at the entrance to the train station, observes the crowds and checks she is not being watched.

The railway station's vaulted ceilings and glazed archways expose its various layers, as though it has been cut away at certain points to expose its workings, the curve of its ribs. She feels as though she is inside some giant beast on display in a museum. She lingers and listens to the conversations of huddled groups in the station's cavernous interior, to the talk of commuters rushing between platforms. She can only hope that Alexis will not have managed to follow her here, so she stands and watches and listens until she is satisfied that he is not there. She is so engrossed in this task that she does not notice the small figure approaching through the crowds until she collides with her, knocking Wren off balance. She looks down into the bright, wide eyes of a young girl and puts a hand out to prevent her from falling on the concourse. They smile at each other and over the girl's shoulder Wren sees a woman hurrying through the crowds towards them.

The girl is staring up at Wren and Wren looks down to find she is still holding the flower from the market. The girl accepts it with a smile.

Stoya, the woman says, angry, out of breath. What have I said about running off? You know how easy it is to become lost.

The woman looks at Wren, wary, and the small girl continues to watch her too. The woman nods a guarded thanks and takes the girl's hand and as they walk away Wren listens to the woman admonish her daughter. The girl turns for a second, waves the flower and then she is gone, absorbed back into the crowd.

Stoya. Wren says it aloud to herself. She likes the idea of becoming Stoya. It seems right that she should take a new name, one from O. It will complete her transformation.

On the noticeboard, there are cards for missing people, lonely hearts, adverts for restaurants and hotels, cheap taxis, casual jobs, furniture and houses for sale. She scans for the cards that advertise rooms for rent. There are perhaps a hundred or so. She looks at each in turn and, when she sees the one she has been looking for, she copies the details into her notebook. Cheap rooms, Porazha, 2650 Zamésche. Cheap is important, though she still has plenty left on the roll of money she took from Cleo. There is no phone number on this card as there is on the others. She looks for other notices in the same area, though this is the only one. She has already decided this is where she is going.

When she has moved away from the board, I approach and remove the card.

FIFTEEN

IT TAKES WREN the rest of the day to locate Zamésche. Every few streets she has to stop to ask for further directions. The address is in a sprawling area she has not visited before. It is a district she imagines will not be on the itinerary of many of the organised tours. When she comes out into the square on which she has been told the boarding house stands, she walks around the small market and watches for a while from beneath the canopy of a fruit stall. Dogs and children range around the edges. To one side of the covered stalls, there are a few tables around which men of all ages play backgammon, draughts, tynyn. Further out from the market, towards a parade that consists mostly of boarded-up shops with grilles covered in graffiti, four girls are playing a game with a long skipping rope. Small brown birds sit on loose telegraph wires strung between the buildings.

She watches three children walk around the edge of the square, heading towards one of the derelict-looking buildings, a concrete tower block the ground floor of which is pock-marked with small holes, as though someone has been taking chips out of the walls. Two of them carry a pair of uncoupled stereo speakers across the cracked ground and a third, a younger child, follows behind trailing smoke from a thin cigarette. They look like a small military unit. The pair out in front are slightly larger than the third. They are trying to maintain boy-swagger while carrying the speakers, though they are slightly too heavy for them to carry easily. The youngest has an androgynous look and Wren cannot be sure but she thinks it is probably a girl. She has a hard look about her. They disappear into the darkness of the building and she hears them shouting in the stairwell.

She takes out her notebook and checks the address though there is no mistaking it when she looks across at the building, which has PORAZHA carved in block capitals above the door. The Porazha is a light-grey concrete building. It seems too large somehow for the area in which it stands. It is taller than the buildings in the surrounding streets, broader too. It speaks of a level of ambition that the district was too weak to support. Many of the windows and doors on the ground floor are bricked up and others are boarded with perforated metal. The upper floors are encased in a huge net, which she presumes is there to catch any falling masonry and to prevent birds from entering the building through the open windows on the top floors, some of which are unglazed, empty eyeholes.

She is walking towards the building when she hears noise from the tower block. The four children are shouting from an open window, and she turns in time to see the two speakers as they drop several storeys and crash to the floor.

Charming, aren't they?

At the doorway to the Porazha, a woman is looking over the square to where the speakers now lie in pieces. The woman is as broad as she is tall and she wears a full-length floral dress.

Do you know who I'd talk to about a room here? Wren says.

The woman looks Wren up and down and leers.

We have rooms, she says. But you don't sound the type.

It is dark inside and Wren takes up little space in the

Porazha's formerly grand entrance hall. With lights and some new furniture, it could almost pass for a functional hotel. Against the back wall there is a dark-wood reception desk and behind this there is a blackboard on which there are messages scrawled in chalk and a nail board with numbered pegs on which hang key fobs. Behind the desk, a gameshow is playing on two televisions that hang from brackets on the wall. The images on the two screens are slightly out of sync and Wren wonders which of them the woman watches.

Maybe I don't sound the type, but I'd still like a room, she says.

The woman shrugs and looks up at the nail board.

I've got one that's just vacated, she says. Not that I think you'll want it. I've got a bed in a shared room too if you want to look at that.

The woman looks put out when Wren asks to see the first room. The Porazha is a huge building and they walk along corridors the ends of which look impossibly far away, all carpeted with threadbare brown and cream swirl carpets.

It was a hotel once, the woman says, as though this is all the explanation that is needed.

She is right, though the Porazha was more than a hotel. It was an institution, one of the best, far from the centre, anonymous and well worth the journey. Some of us remember discos in these ballrooms. We recall the cocktails that Mizheil, who we all suspected was actually one of us, mixed white Russians, screwdrivers, martinis with the bitterest of olives, cocktails that had no name and were based on whatever spirits and fruit juices he had managed to get hold of. He was a magician, Mizheil.

Who else stays here? Wren asks.

All sorts. You'll meet them soon enough if you stay. You won't be here long. Like I said, you're not the type.

The woman unlocks a door with a key attached to a key fob.

The room is large and a plate-glass window dominates one wall and looks back towards the centre of O. It reminds her of the room Alexis had shown her opposite the sculpture park and she loves it immediately.

Bathroom's down the corridor, the woman says. There's running water, and electricity sometimes. No one really knows how it works and it's sporadic, which made opportunists of us all. Heating is non-existent, but we have some electric heaters you can rent, which aren't without their drawbacks obviously.

Her tone has shifted from one of mild aggression to that of someone who regrets the situation but is resigned to it.

Wren surveys the room. The single bed looks small against the wall. At least the bed has been made. Next to the bed there is a table constructed of magazines on which sits a small lamp. The sleeve of a jumper looks as though it is making a bid to escape from a partly open cupboard door. It looks to her as though the last occupant has stepped out and has simply not returned. Against the same wall there are two tallboys, one of which is missing a leg and is propped up by more magazines. By the door is a stove and cupboard that contains a few stained, chipped plates and bowls.

Is there not someone else living here? Wren asks.

She stopped paying her rent, so if you want it, it's yours, the woman says. Do what you like with anything she left. Do you want to take it or not?

It is close enough to the curfew now for Wren to agree to pay up front a week in advance for the room. The woman waits while Wren fishes out some notes from the toe end of the pair of tights in her bag and exchanges the money for a form, which she signs under the name Stoya. She gives her mother's house on Omniastriste as her previous address.

Passport, the woman says, holding out a hand.

She is not giving this woman her passport.

I can bring it to you later, she says.

The woman raises an eyebrow and keeps her hand out. Wren hands over notes until the woman nods and puts her other hand on the small pile they have made.

Later then, she says. She ticks a box on her form and hands over a fob. This is the only key. When you leave, you give the key to me and I hang it on the board. When you come back, I give you the key again. You understand?

Wren nods and the woman leaves. One of the tallboys is empty and Wren folds the few clothes she has brought with her onto its shelves. She stows her bag beneath the bed. The second tallboy contains women's clothes that she presumes belong to the room's previous occupant. Later, she tries these clothes on, frayed purple cords and knitted jumpers that come down to her knees and which have holes in the arms and bodies. They are similar to the clothes she has seen students wearing. She will add them to her new wardrobe. She hides her passport in one of the tallboys.

On closer inspection, she sees the metal-framed window is shared with the room next door and is divided by a partition wall. The room must have been enormous originally, she thinks. There are no curtains at the window but a large sheet is pinned to one side of the window that she presumes stretches its length when it is pulled across. The other three walls are a mix of bare concrete, ripped wallpaper and paint that has been applied in patches. She should be depressed by it. Cleo would have had the room redecorated and furnished before she moved in, complementing shades of paint, everything tasteful and matching. Cleo would not have been here in the first place. Wren sits on the bed and flicks through the magazines at the top of the pile. They are fashion magazines and the room's previous inhabitant had ringed outfits, annotated pages with her thoughts and notes.

Wren sits on the bed and leans against the badly fitted partition wall. The wall gives slightly. Her neighbour's cigarette smoke seeps through the gap where the partition meets the window. She can hear one side of this woman's phone conversation. It concerns the breakdown of the woman's family and the circumstances that have led to her leaving her home for what she describes as a terrible shithole. The woman's partner in the conversation is her mother, Wren guesses, or perhaps her mother-in-law, and there are long periods of silence during which Wren assumes the conversation has finished, only for it to start again, a kind of rolling battle that goes on late into the night.

Outside, the city takes on its evening guise. When Wren turns the lamp off, light bleeds through from the room next door and she can see reflected movement in the window. She can feel her neighbour pacing through the wall. She inhales the other woman's cigarette smoke second hand and listens to her continuing and increasingly irate phone call. She wonders if Alexis has returned home to the burnt, soaked mass of photographs and negatives, what his reaction will be. She wonders again if he will look for her and if so if he will be able to find her. It would be difficult, she thinks, especially if she has managed to leave Hereckl without him noticing. O is vast.

Amid the conversations and arguments that go on all evening she closes her eyes and sleeps to the sound of murmurs that creep through the paper-thin walls.

SIXTEEN

ALEXIS'S BREATH, HEAVY in her ear. Rhythmic. Metronomic. It takes her a few moments to realise that he is not there.

For the first few days, she has to force herself to leave the building. Every few steps she is certain she hears shutter clicks hidden in the street sounds, and that every flash of light is a lens catching the sun. There is nothing to be gained by thinking this way. Alexis cannot have followed her, she is sure of it.

She has crossed twelve names off her list of possibles and there are still thirty more to go, all of them in streets she has not yet found. It occurs to her that she could do things differently now she is not with Alexis. To hell with his caution about maps. She will create her own.

She buys a notebook of the type a tourist might buy, with a deep red sheen and the *O'chian* coat of arms embossed on the front cover. She marks the Porazha in the centre of the first double page spread and begins to sketch the streets immediately around it. It is slow work but it is important that she should get this right.

Over the next few days, the pages of her notebook grow thick with blue lines that spread out from the Porazha. She applies the full weight of her concentration to the streets and the people around her. It is a way of taming the chaos of a city, a way of keeping herself grounded.

Across the course of the next week, her map fills several

pages. She discovers three more streets on which there are families named Donietz-husj, though each one is a dead end. The first two are houses that seem to be owned or rented by single, elderly women, and the third is a young family. Even so, she feels as though she has achieved something that in all her time with Alexis she had not.

She buys the *Morning O* each day and scans for references to protests and riots, and though there are none, she is certain there is a subtext to some of the articles that she does not understand.

Aside from the sighing and pacing and the cigarette smoke, Wren hears little of her window neighbour. This neighbour only ever has one visitor, a man with whom she often argues late into the night. These arguments are not personal, but political. Her boyfriend, if that's who he is, is trying to convince her to leave O and make a new start with him while it is still possible. The couple who live in the room on the other side of Wren's work during the day. She hears them between the hours of six and seven when, she presumes, they eat breakfast together and then again between nine and ten in the evening. A table, she guesses, from the clink of glass and cutlery, is set against the wall. If all else is quiet, it is possible to hear them muttering grace. Above her lives a man who suffers from insomnia. She often hears him pacing the floor above, usually between twelve and four in the morning. After a while, she gets used to the sound of it and she falls asleep to the metronome of his footsteps.

Zamésche is alive in the same way a garden that was once well tended and has now been left to revert to the state to which it aspires is alive, untamed and raucous. The market in the square outside the Porazha springs up and disappears

133

to a timetable she does not understand. Six in the morning, four in the afternoon. Midday until one. Then there will be no market at all for several days.

In the streets behind the Porazha there are workshops of all kinds – metal workers, jewellers, carpenters – restaurants and cinemas with no signs to announce they are there, and a basement shop where novels, cassettes, and pornography that has been smuggled in through the port can be exchanged for a small fee.

Officially, of course, we shouldn't have to do this any more, the woman who runs this shop tells her. But it's like any way of life, it's difficult to give up, and no one quite trusts that things won't return to the way they were.

Here too it is possible to climb up onto the roof. The Porazha is taller than Alexis's apartment block in Herekl and from here, on a clear day, Wren can make out the mountains of the interior in the far distance. From here, she watches the sun set between layers of cloud, the rooftops across the city ablaze in a way so unlike that of the early morning that it might be a different city entirely. She looks towards the Kesibyr from here, too. It catches the morning sun and, at times, reflects a beam of light. At these times it resembles a lighthouse, and she wonders who it is warning and of what. When the wind blows down from the mountains it takes her to places beyond the city.

She continues her exploration of the city. She walks slowly, taking in everything she can and stopping every hour or so to add new details to her maps in the red notebook. She crosses narrow footbridges and as she passes houses she makes a mental note of each of the brass plaques that announce the family names of those within: Frederick, Bétle-husj, Shlestinà,

Kitsch, Kara-husj and, less often, Donietz-husj. She admires the deep steps that sweep up to the doors and the doors themselves, each painted in a rich, deep hue. She resists the temptation to run up the steps and press the cracked ivory doorbells. Through an open window she hears a piano playing a piece she recognises and stops to listen. It is Chopin, a piece she has heard her mother play innumerable times. It pulls at her heart. The playing is confident and delicate. Wren can see in her mind's eye the practised fingers moving as though entirely of their own accord and realises she is imagining the piece played by her mother. Despite everything, she misses Cleo. The music stops mid-phrase and she emerges from her dream and continues along the street. The music inspires in her a sort of unease, and as she walks she allows herself to slip for a few minutes into a sort of melancholy.

Further down, at one of the large restaurants, starched linen tablecloths are being stretched over tables, cutlery polished and placed down by precise, confident hands. The lunch service has not yet begun and the waiters and waitresses have the floor. One of the waiters looks up as if he senses her looking in and smiles. A short way on, a car pulls alongside her and the man in the driver's seat leans across and tells her, out of the open window, to get into the car and when she says she will not the man calls her a whore and swerves back out into the traffic.

SEVENTEEN

TIDES RISE AND fall and the waterways, for the most part, do their job. Once more, the houseboats do not crack under the weight of ice and although the winter storms damage the sea walls, they remain standing for another year and we silently thank those giants of ages past who created such solid, immovable things. Ice gives way to rain and the streets become indistinguishable from the rivers. Small, bright flowers start to show themselves again, on the ground between the tram tracks. The trams themselves gleam.

Wren, out of the reach of her mother and Alexis, reminds me of myself as a child, running the gauntlet of stevedores at the docks with a gang to reach the breakwater and hurling ourselves off naked into the freezing grey sea, only to haul ourselves out and jump back in again. She is reckless. She is unaware of the danger in which she is putting herself. Either that or she does not care at all who sees what she is doing. We are practised at turning a blind eye, though I cannot control what others see, what others notice, and I worry for her.

Wren adds to her room a full-length mirror, a hat stand, and a table and chair she finds abandoned in the scrub ground behind the Porazha. The Porazha is generous in this way.

She sustains herself with an almost religious zeal, repeating to herself that what she is doing is important work, that she is making valuable discoveries about the city, that there is no time to lose. She scribbles in the notebook until there is no space left. She buys another notebook, a larger one this time.

She always thought she would rise late when her time was her own, that once she no longer had to care for Cleo, she would languish and the days would spread out in front of her. But she wakes early and when she does it is with new purpose. Even if she does not find her father, she will know the city as well as anyone can know a place. She will know it intimately. Even in the badly partitioned room she feels freer, like a sapling hardening to the world.

By March she starts to reach the outer eastern edges of O where the city fades into farmland and then scrub or thick forest. If we had maps in O this site would not appear on them. If she feels uneasy here, it is because the scrubland over which she now walks is the site of a massacre of two hundred and fifty-seven, mainly men and boys, on 23 April 1988. There is no record of this event other than in the memories of the way a certain uncle used to fill the room with plumes of rose tobacco, or the way a mother threaded her fingers through her son's hair. The bodies of those interred here, some as little as three feet below Wren's shoes, are barely decomposed. We neither acknowledge nor admit that this event and others like it occurred here, that our neighbours and friends were complicit, that there are those among our own ranks involved or, if not involved, who observed and said nothing. It will be some years before these bodies are acknowledged, before guilt is assigned and apportioned.

Ask about O and we will tell you the stories of our city's founding fathers, the impregnable city state. We will tell you of the failed invasions, coups, the rise and fall of dynasties, though do not expect us to be so forthcoming about our more recent past. Do not ask about the plastered-over bullet holes on the walls of apartment blocks nor those that remain on the steps of the courts. We will not tell you that despite the fact we protected ourselves from invasion for so long, we were not able to protect ourselves from ourselves.

While looking for her father, Wren traces the waterways, the tramways both used and abandoned, her favourite routes through the city. She maps the way in which light falls in different parts of the city at different times of day on walls that are crumbling into the Meret. She pays particular attention to unpopulated and abandoned places. They are like breathing spaces, pockets within the city in which she can feel safe. She charts abandoned cinemas and swimming pools, former factories that appear to have been forgotten even by the squatters, houses that are clearly fronts for something else entirely.

Sometimes, she will see a face like her own staring out at her from windows, from statues, paintings, etchings. It ought to be reassuring, she thinks, to see herself reflected back. It ought to give her a sense of belonging, she thinks.

For a moment, standing by the river in a half-sleep state, she entertains the thought that the Meret is a sentient thing, that O itself is overlaid on some ancient consciousness that tolerates the buildings that have been placed over the nest sites of birds and the labyrinth of streets that has been placed over the labyrinth of tracks made by boar and deer centuries and millennia before the first people of O created their own routes through the forest.

On most days she follows the same routine. She wakes early and wraps herself in her bedsheet. She enjoys the darkness and the stillness of the former hotel at that time. Even the insomniac in the room above has become still by this time and she can feel she has the building to herself. She stands at the window and notes the changes in the scene outside from the previous day.

She might notice upward of a hundred small differences in those few moments in the morning and file them away. On the morning of the twentieth of March, the rain is heavy and seems endless. The sheets the woman in the apartment directly opposite has hung from her balcony are soaked through and it looks for a moment as if she has filled the space with concrete. A single grey sock hangs next to the sheets and on the window-sill of the kitchen alongside are two unwashed cups that were there the day before. One of the cups has been turned and she can see, through the rain-streaked window, a chip on its rim. In the road, among the cars that are used and those that are abandoned, there is one that was not there yesterday. It is brown and boxy and one of the door panels has been re-placed with another that is not quite the same shade of brown and there is plastic sheeting in place of the triangular window in the passenger-side door that has gathered a pool of water where it is not stretched tight. Its roof is coated in bird shit. This is the closest she has come to seeing me. I resolve to take more care. The only figure she sees in the street is a woman wearing a long grey coat with the hood up, a woman who I suspect is watching me. This is only a tradesman's instinct. The woman glances at me, then looks up at the window briefly as if she senses Wren watching, and walks on.

Later, when the rain stops, Wren buys a roll of white paper and uses it to cover one of the walls in her room. She sharpens a pencil and draws a faint sketch onto it, the Kesibyr, in the centre of the wall, an anchor, a centre point. To one side, she draws the small section of the city she knows well, the points between her mother's house and Alexis's apartment and the surrounding areas, the docks and the market, the library. In another area she draws the Porazha and the streets around the boarding house. She transfers the maps from her notebooks, the streets on which she has searched for her father, the exact points at which she has not found him. It is as much an exercise in grounding herself as it is in putting her mark on the place. It can only be an improvement on the current decoration of the room. When she has finished the map, the city resembles a series of islands connected by thin road bridges, by the ribbons of the Meret.

She works on her map most days, though the more she works on it the more she realises she needs to rewrite routes created previously. She has made errors, misjudgements, miscalculations. There are roads and turnings she had not noticed before, whole buildings she somehow walked by without seeing. She is surprised at the number of times she still becomes lost, at how quickly the city becomes strange and she has to retreat to streets she knows well. It is not the places themselves that are the problem – she has several areas of the city well documented, she is sure of that. It is the connective tissue that is the problem, the big picture.

Sometimes, she feels certain that her father is close by. She can sense him in the architecture, in the curve of the road or the river and as her map expands she skirts the areas in which she lived before. At night, she traces the possible journeys he takes on her map with a finger. She imagines both of their paths simultaneously, close but never quite meeting.

At times she misses Alexis. She misses the smell of the chemicals he used for developing film, the washing line of prints drying above the bath, the basin, the bed. She can picture him now, breaking his camera down into its component parts and then as he unwraps the cloth bundle that contains the fine brushes and pipettes he uses to clear dust from the lenses.

She tries to put him out of her mind, but she often finds herself looking for him in the street. She sees elements of him reflected in other men, in their features and mannerisms. She hopes he is unable to concentrate on the images he is being paid to capture, that he expects at any moment to see her walking by or emerging from one of the buildings on which he has his camera trained. She hopes that he obsesses, that he stays behind the lens for longer than he needs to, in the hope he will find a clue, that when he is not working he retreats to his darkroom and even there he cannot forget her.

It is well into April before she realises that the expectation she will see Alexis every time she leaves the protection of the Porazha, in the shadow of a door on the opposite side of the road or recognise his face in a crowd, has fallen away a little.

The Porazha hums. It vibrates. Aside from the few families and loners, the majority of people Wren sees in the corridors look like students. Sometimes, she sees signs of gatherings in the otherwise empty rooms, groups involved in serious, dense conversations, though what they are discussing she has no idea. She has no idea of how these meetings are organised either until she sees scraps of paper with dates and room numbers pinned to certain walls on certain corridors. Wren makes a note of the time on one of them and when it arrives she dresses in the clothes of her room's former occupant and joins.

Room 0375, Wren discovers, is in the Porazha's basement,

in one of the former hotel's now-empty kitchens, the equipment having long since been sold off in small batches, the ovens and refrigerators sold to furnish other kitchens, the pans redistributed or melted down to convert to other uses, as stills or – we worry – light arms. There are still some in this city who have the kind of knowledge necessary to do this, though these individuals are watched carefully and none of them is present at the meeting Wren attends.

She wonders if these were the sorts of meetings her father sat in on or presided over, but she cannot picture him here among the students. They are disorganised and talk over each other. No one questions her appearance there. The discussions that animate these groups are hardly radical. They are discussing methods for posting their messages. The students appear to be in two camps: those who favour graffiti and those who prefer flyering. The latter contend that graffiti is essentially an act of violence. It is an imposition, one of them says, whereas flyering, as a less permanent statement, covers the bases of being both subversive and essentially non-violent.

One conversation revolves entirely around the best type of adhesive for posting flyers. Some favour wheat paste, whereas others argue that glue is no alternative to packing tape for ease of posting and that it involves less risk. Their conversations are rife with speculation and conspiracy theories. One serious-looking young man claims the police have installed tiny cameras into each copy machine at the university, and someone in the depths of one of the city's administrative buildings is going through each photocopied item, gathering evidence, though one of the others claims that he has taken one of the machines apart and found no cameras within and the young man shrugs gnomically and says they would have to agree to differ on it. In any case, he says, he does not make any copies on campus, so the point is moot.

At the end of the meeting, a young man stands at the front of the room and hands out a badly produced zine and they file out. It is harmless stuff: recipes, photographs of statues and buildings, poetry, short stories. Anything of interest, she figures, will be hidden deep in some code they have developed.

Around this time, Wren's money runs out. She approaches Letzsena on the reception desk, who tells her there are several girls at the Porazha who clean at night. They are always looking for more, she says. Wren can work at night and the rest of her time she will be free to do as she wants. She will be picked up by minibus at the entrance just after the curfew kicks in and taken to the offices of government, to administrative buildings, and returned just before the curfew ends. All she needs do, if she is interested, Letzsena tells her, is to be in the reception area at ten that evening.

The pay is poor but rent at the Porazha is minimal and the drive through the city at night makes it worth the tiredness. A van collects her and a few others shortly after the bells sound and they collect other small groups in districts across the city. The van crawls through the streets and O seems a different place entirely. The streets look older in the post-curfew quietness than the ones she knows, and the twisting paths between the factories, offices and units, the purpose of which she has no idea, darken further through the tinted van windows. At times, she is sure the driver takes a longer route than is necessary even to navigate through the city's confusions.

Most of the women with whom Wren works sleep in their seats as soon as they set off.

We are stealing back time, one of them tells her.

She finds she cannot sleep on these journeys. At first she watches for patrols, for the groups of men with dogs on leads whom she has always assumed enforce the curfew, but there is no one. She stares from the window and watches for the headlights to catch foxes or dogs in their beams. The girl who sits next to Wren in the van tells her she saw a bear once, wandering alone through the streets, though Wren is not sure she believes her.

They work through until four the next morning in offices and empty apartments, halls and concert venues, vacuuming, polishing, cleaning, and later, the van returns to take them back. It drops them on the steps of the Porazha just as the curfew lifts. Wren likes these journeys, when the city is at its emptiest.

As she walks silent corridors in the earliest hours of the morning, she sometimes thinks of Alexis and the way he had talked about his work, moving like a ghost through the city.

The small army of cleaners is watched by cameras mounted on the ceilings and by supervisors who make a half-hearted patrol while the others clean, vacuum, scrub desks and floors.

Around this time, Wren has the feeling she is being watched again. There is a tangible shift in the atmosphere around the Porazha. She believed, until this point, that she had perfected the art of being unseen. It is not so difficult. She looks, or so she has been told several times, pure O and, if she does not talk too much, she can pass pretty much as having lived in the city her whole life.

A woman, passing her in one of the Porazha's broad corridors, does a double-take as they draw level, though when

Wren turns, the woman looks confused as though she cannot quite place her, and moves on. A boy of about seventeen who is walking in the opposite direction to her on a long straight road that leads out towards the eastern edge of the city raises a hand and seems on the verge of talking when he catches himself, apologises and moves on. She is unnerved and, as she continues, she looks to check that he is not following, though he keeps walking and she does not see him again. This feels different to the unasked-for attention any woman walking alone attracts. There is a sort of half-recognition for which she cannot account. She looks at herself in mirrored windows but she can see nothing different about her appearance, nothing that would draw any more attention to her than usual. She tries to put the thought out of her head. As the week wears on though, she finds herself counting the people who show more than usual interest in her.

As she approaches the sprawling mass of industrial units in this part of the city she begins to relax again. The feeling fades and she is able to convince herself that she is being sensitive to something that is not actually there. She wonders if it is paranoia or a trick of the mind, a product of being so long in her own company.

When Letzsena jokes that she will be increasing Wren's rent seeing as how she is famous now, she thinks at first that it is the receptionist's attempt at a joke. It is not until she goes to buy cigarettes from the kiosk close to the Porazha that she sees the photograph. The woman who runs the kiosk holds a copy of the New East out to her as she approaches. She tells Wren she has been waiting for her to come by all day and the day before too. Wren takes the magazine, shakes her head and passes it back.

There is certainly a likeness but it is not me, she says.

The woman laughs and when she hands over Wren's Vaniks she insists that Wren should take the magazine too. She has told all her friends, she says, that she knows the woman in the photograph everyone is talking about. Wren puts the magazine beneath her arm and tries to forget it until she reaches her room. Even then as she places the magazine on the bed unopened and stares at it she cannot connect herself with the image of the woman on the cover, though she knows logically that it is her. She does not want to look, in any case, though she knows that her not looking will not affect whether other people see it.

The cover image is partially covered by the magazine's title and various headlines, so it is easy to imagine that it is not really herself, though when she flicks through to the main article she almost drops the magazine. The article is titled 'The New Authentic'. She scans for Alex's credit, though there is no mention of him. It looks like it could be one of his, though, a photograph she missed.

It's not me, she says aloud to herself. There's a likeness but it's not me.

Wren's head spins. She feels the city constrict. She stares at the photograph. Though it is clearly her, she cannot connect herself with the image of the woman.

The young woman pictured is looking back over her shoulder. The image is cropped and the only clothing visible is the collar of her coat. Two strands of dark hair cross her forehead. The woman's face, her eyes and lips, are in sharp focus. One of her hands is raised and her lips are slightly parted, as though she is reading aloud the words, testing them. The look on her face is one of pure concentration and something else that conveys the sense that she is in the process of discovering something through the articulation of these words. And though Wren recognises the woman in the photograph as corresponding to her in every way, she still cannot reconcile herself with the image.

We will later argue over the photograph. It is thought by some that her expression matches that of the lost Daughter of O, though many of us consider her expression to be accusatory. Perhaps it will be judged differently in time, but right now, as we embark on a new millennium, the feeling that rises in us as we look at the photograph of Wren Lithgow is one of shame. For others, it is inflammatory, for over the following few days we will receive orders to find the girl in the photograph.

The article proclaims the photograph is evidence of a new aesthetic. The feature is bolstered by commentaries from artists in other fields – writers, fine artists, sculptors. In keeping with this aesthetic, the photographer will not be named, one of the artists interviewed is quoted as saying. It is ironic. Wren can see Alexis's fingerprints on the photograph as clearly as if he were the subject.

She needs to think. She stops at the cinema and buys a ticket for the next viewing without looking at what the film is. She needs the darkness, the anonymity the cinema offers, the calm of the stalls. There are few other people in the cinema. A middle-aged couple kissing urgently on the back row, two men who sit four rows apart from each other. It is an old film. Black and white. Badly dubbed. Wren switches off from the action on screen. She lets the images flash in front of her and does not take them in.

Over the next few days, the photograph runs on the

front cover of the two main city newspapers, *Morning O* and *Evening O*, and in the pages of the paper of the dockers' union and later in the few foreign-language magazines. Wren thinks on it, how far it goes, through whose hands the image will pass, whether people whose lives she has shared briefly in other cities will double-take at it, if they will wonder why it seems familiar. She pulls her bag from beneath her bed and begins to stuff her clothes into it. She is not ready for this. She packs and unpacks the bag.

Wren becomes increasingly afraid of being recognised in the street. When she does leave the Porazha, she pulls her hat down low. She goes out now only for short periods and spends most of her time in her room in the hope that it will all blow over.

As the fear grows, she spends much of her time fantasising over the revenge she would like to wreak on Alexis. She creates elaborate scenarios in which he is injured. She stares at the map and imagines for herself two goons who walk the streets looking for Alexis and she ensures that at some point their paths will cross. In some of these scenarios, they argue and Alexis leaves, shaken, and in others, the two men threaten him or hit him with meat-like fists until his face becomes a bloody pulp. When she emerges from this protracted thought, she realises she needs to confront him, to find out why he has done this.

There is no answer at Alexis's building, so Wren presses all the call buttons on the board and someone, annoyed at the buzzing, unlocks the door. There is no reply either when she gets to the door of Alexis's apartment though she shouts his name and bangs on his door. When she is convinced he is not simply ignoring her, she goes up to the rooftop to wait for him to return.

She lights a cigarette and sits on the low wall and shortly after this she registers movement in the film studio opposite. When she looks across the divide she sees several men walking around the studio. One of them pushes over a lighting rig, another begins to tear posters from the walls. At first, she assumes this is part of a film, a scene being rehearsed, though when she sees one of the men removing film from a camera, unspooling it onto the floor, she realises they are destroying the studio. She moves back, away from the ledge. They are practised, these men, systematic, careful. She sees the film-makers arrive and wants to warn them, though they are inside the building before she can shout down, and in any case, she does not want to draw attention to herself. The next time she sees the couple is as they come into frame in the studio. Two men are holding them, arms behind their backs. They hold the couple there to watch the destruction of their studio. The whole process takes ten minutes, perhaps, and when it is over, they march the filmmakers out of the studio. The street is filling and there are several people passing, though no one pays attention to the pair as they are bundled into a car parked on the street outside.

She is suddenly afraid of this city and she leaves without trying Alexis's door again.

EIGHTEEN

THE CAFÉS IN the streets beyond are shuttered. Elsewhere, across the city, families are rising. They walk on thick carpets, lay tables for breakfast, anchored to their own lives by the weight of heavy cutlery. They walk around these houses with the confidence of children who are certain of the stability of the walls of their houses, of their impregnability.

The memory of the sun's heat is as slow to return as heat itself. Commuters and hustlers alike continue to wear their long coats long after they need them, and their woollen hats and scarves, until the sweat runs down their backs. Seabirds watch workmen on abseil ropes as they fill the gaps where waves have swept away large chunks of concrete from the sea walls over winter. The first cruise ship of the year arrives, though it is mostly empty. Only the hardiest tourists disembark with their tall backpacks. Other passengers watch from behind thick glass on the upper decks, unimpressed, for the ship to continue to its next stop.

Reasonable men carrying the reasonable requests of their superiors visit the offices of newspapers and radio stations. They do so in person, to remind the broadcasters and journalists of the longstanding relationship between the media and the state, to remind them of the way things work. They do not threaten or bully; they explain that it is important that the Parade of Lights is well attended, that though the year is still young the people of O should begin to prepare. There is no need to explain the consequences of their friendly advice being ignored. Memories of some things do not fade.

Wren rises through a dream of a fox that is pouncing again and again, burying its front paws and head into deep, undisturbed snow for a mouse that trembles somewhere beneath. When she wakes she lies face up and watches the blackness swim and it takes her a while to shake the feeling that any minute the paws or bared teeth of a huge fox will come crashing through the ceiling. She rises and pulls out a pair of tights from her drawer and uses them to stop up some of the gaps in the window. She aches. She resists the urge to return to bed, pulls on a jumper, lies on the floor and tries to stretch the cold from her limbs. She watches her arms and legs as she extends them in the semi-darkness and they feel foreign to her, places she once visited that are now strange and distant.

During the nights, Wren is driven from one anonymous place to the next, where she cleans until the van returns and they move on to the next.

By this time, the photograph has gone international. The mystery of who she is only adds to the intrigue around it. I continue to watch, to bide my time. There may be others who are watching her now but they will be uncertain as to the value they ought to ascribe to information concerning her. We are well used to weighing the currency of information but, as yet, no one says anything. She perplexes us, bemuses, discomfits, alarms, this girl, who is at once of O and not of O.

The posters Wren had seen when she arrived in O reappear and in greater numbers than before, scrappy photocopied sheets in high contrast black and white, on fences and bus stops, on the walls of bakeries and government buildings, on railway hoardings and fences. She sees them everywhere now pasted to walls and lampposts. A close-up of the image of Wren's face with the slogan SHE SEES YOU and then a name, often one she has read in the newspaper – they are politicians, administrators, military commanders. When Wren next passes the same way, the posters have almost always been removed in the interim, or all that is left of them are parallel streaks of paper where the paste still holds.

Questions about the new Daughter of O continue to spread. Who is this girl who seems to epitomise the city? Who seems to capture something that is, as yet, only in the air? Who seems at once of this time and timeless? We listen in to conversations on tapped phone lines in which these questions are asked over and again. We listen on devices that amplify the voices of those fifty metres away, even through glass – what marvellous technology we now have access to. At what point these questions turn to speculation, turn to conjecture, turn to fact, we cannot say with any precision. Stories move in mysterious ways. We cannot tell precisely when the Daughter of O becomes conflated with the girl in the photograph. Of the point at which our paymasters become interested in her, we are more certain.

There are men looking for you, Letzsena says as Wren enters the reception one afternoon in late August. They are showing your photograph around. Do you recognise this girl? they say. I told them, yes, I recognise her well. She is the Daughter of O. This did not make them happy.

Why would you help me? Wren asks.

It is a natural instinct, is it not, Letzsena says, to deny? The van will be here soon – you will need to change out of those good clothes.

Wren's map takes on new purpose. She works and reworks sections of the city, shifts whole areas and leaves space for parts of O she knows she has still not explored. It stretches the length of the wall now and she tries to work out how much of the city she has covered. She has moved her bed away from the wall to incorporate its most southerly reaches. It crowds her walls and her head. She thinks of little else. In the hours between returning from cleaning and her daytime walks she sleeps little. She goes over earlier sections, rescales, resituates streets she now knows lead onto others, alters and remoulds the rivers' curves. In sections where the wallpaper has peeled away and the rough concrete is exposed, she sands it back as best she can.

Now when she stands with her back to the window in her room it feels sometimes that in her map she is close to uncovering a grand design and at other times she feels there is no value to it at all and she despairs. She searches for patterns in what she has drawn, clues for areas she has overlooked, but sees none. It is at those times she considers painting over the mural.

There is a point at which she wonders if the city will stretch beyond the edges of the wall.

When it grows dark, Wren closes the curtains and turns the bedside light towards the wall to illuminate the section of the map on which she is working. It is an important part of her day, this ritual of transferring the notes she has made. A way of grounding herself, while everything around her is falling apart.

NINETEEN

CLEO RETURNS TO O in September, almost exactly a year after she and Wren arrived. There are adverts in the papers, on the radio. Cleo is to play a one-off performance of Schubert's *Winterreise*.

Her visit, her one-off performance, is timed for the week that runs up to the great Parade of Lights for which preparations are well underway: bunting criss-crosses the streets, police practise their crowd-control methods, bands practise new march tunes composed specifically for this event.

Wren sees Cleo's return for what it is. It is her way of saying she wants to talk, a chance to change her daughter's mind. She will expect Wren to attend. And though Wren has no interest in joining in with whatever game Cleo is playing, she knows she will go. She misses Cleo. She feels sad for the way things ended. Not guilty, just sad. Cleo is right. It is time for her to leave. If, as Letzsena has said, there are people searching for her now, O is not safe, and though she does not want to admit it to herself, her mother was right. It is not safe for her here.

It is a strange experience, to walk into the concert hall with everyone else. As a child, Wren was expected to make herself scarce while Cleo performed and Wren realises that, aside from in photographs, in rehearsals and at home, she has rarely ever seen her mother perform.

The couple in the seats to her right are talking about Cleo when Wren sits down. They are fans, obsessives, the type who will talk even if they are repeating the same thoughts they have held about Cleo for years, even if it is a repeat of the conversation they have just had. They are the type who expect that everyone feels the same way they do. Cleo inspires this reaction in some people.

She's a mystery, the woman says, implicating Wren into the conversation as she takes her seat. Even after all these years. How she does what she does. And her hands.

God, her hands. It's like watching ballet.

It's erotic.

It's funny what people read into her performances, Wren thinks.

Did you ever find out why she left the last time?

Wren shakes her head.

I never got the refund for the tickets we had.

Maybe that's what this is. An apology.

Wren wants to tell them that her mother does not do apologies.

Still, to see her play, it is a religious experience, the man says, sotto voce. The orchestra has finished tuning up.

Cleo walks out onto the stage with a suited man, a tenor Wren does not recognise. Wren's stomach lurches. The singer lifts his hand to the audience and the applause builds. Cleo sits and smiles, a complicit, professional smile, though she is watching the audience, perhaps scanning for Wren. As she puts her hands to the keyboard, she closes her eyes now and sways as the sound rises and falls around her.

A few minutes in, Wren looks round at those faces around her, staring up at the stage, bright with tears. They are genuinely moved, she thinks and she wonders what memories the music is evoking in them.

When the performance comes to a close, there is a pause, a collective holding of breath across the room. The applause arrives in waves and is accompanied by the stamping of feet and the whole room shakes. As the applause rises again, Cleo thanks the conductor, bows to the orchestra and then to the audience, the consummate professional.

It is not the piece itself that makes me cry, the woman next to her says when it is over and she has recovered herself. It is the playing. Were you not moved by it?

As she says this, the woman's tears start to fall again, staining her silk dress.

I am there too, at the very back of the stalls and on the wooden seats in the gods where there is no view of the stage at all. Our paymasters do not like us to get too comfortable. And even my world-weary eyes fill with tears at the sheer beauty and grief contained within those cascading notes. I am certain that many of those glassy-eyed faces around me are among the ranks of which I am a member. There is an apocryphal story in the intelligence community that, at any football match or parade, half the spectators will be watching the action on the pitch or in the street and the other half will be watching each other. We are aware that many of the reports we write may relate to other members of our community. In this way, the different arms of state security keep tabs on each other. In answer to the age-old question, it is the watchmen who watch the watchmen; they are just, perhaps, not aware that this is what they are doing.

As the crowds head for the exits, Wren walks to the artists' door to the left of the stage, where she is shown through. She is, as she thought, expected.

Cleo is in her dressing room. She is pacing and when Wren enters she flings herself at her daughter and holds her, though Wren holds her hands by her sides, her fists clenched.

You've changed your hair, Cleo says, pulling back. I barely recognise you.

They face each other. Cleo pours Wren a glass though Wren ignores it. There is an Italian magazine on the dressing table. They have used Wren's photograph on the front cover.

You've been noticed, Cleo says. I had to come back for you. You must come back with me.

Wren is about to say yes, she will go away with Cleo, but Cleo holds a hand up to stop her. She has rehearsed this, Wren can tell.

There are things you don't know, Cleo says.

Like what? Wren remains standing. She had been about to agree, though now she pauses.

I will tell you the whole thing, Cleo says. If you come with me. I'm not going to hide it from you. Just promise you'll come back with me.

Cleo looks about ready to fall into one of her rants. She should not have come. This is harder than she thought it would be.

Wren turns to leave.

Just hear me out, Cleo says. She is pleading now. Five minutes. That's all. Listen.

Wren hovers at the door for a moment and then sits on the arm of a sofa. From there, Cleo looks as though she is conducting a whole argument in her head.

Say what you've got to say, Wren says.

Okay, I'm just going to start, she says.

Cleo breathes deeply. She looks almost unrecognisable from the pianist who stepped onto the stage.

I studied here, in O, she says. The city had one of the best conservatoires in Europe. I was here three months before I met Illy. Of course, I didn't tell my parents about him.

I was seventeen. Illy was a student at the university. He was involved in everything. I completed my studies and began to tour, though I came back here often enough to see him, to see if the thing we had together when I was studying was still there. He asked me to marry him and I said no, but that I would make O my home, if he could cope with me travelling. I was going to play all the great cities – I knew that, even then – though I would always come back to him. He said that he would have to settle for that. He was sure I would become like all the other artists who came here and fell in love with O and stayed.

We began to rent an apartment together in Symic and for a while we lived on the money I earned. And then the fighting started, in the north. I ought to have left then, when it started, though it seemed as though it was going to be a temporary thing. Illy told me there had been skirmishes before and they always blew over. You never think it is going to happen to you. You rationalise it. You never think that you will get caught up in something as big as war. And it was only a small war. It was small and it was far away and it would not affect us. There was talk of disturbances in the newspapers, and we listened to reports of fighting on the radio, of crackdowns and the reorganisation of neighbourhoods but it seemed contained and far away. Illy asked me several times to leave and to come back when it was safer, and while there were a thousand reasons I should have gone – they had closed the concert halls by then and the theatres, the opera, as part of emergency measures – we both thought it was a temporary state of affairs. They closed the borders, to contain the arms that were arriving for the rebels, we were told. We were in the city.

It was a beautiful part of the city, where we lived. We were proud of our garden. Even after they closed the concert halls, I walked to work and in the summer or at the weekends we would walk to Illy's brother's house. He lived a mile from us.

She talks about their ordinary life: her family, Illy's studies, the protests they attended, the many friends they had across the city, the flowers in the verges along the many roads that connected the district in which she lived to others, flowers for which O was well known.

Wren dreads what is to come and even though she knows it is going to be bad, she is unprepared.

The fighting was far away at first. We read about it in the papers. We listened to news reports in the evenings and it felt like the fighting was happening in another place, another country. And even when it came closer, we were told we would be protected, that it would not affect us. We were told to carry on as normal. There were soldiers on the street by then and even then they told us it did not affect us. The soldiers were there to protect us. We were good people. We had nothing to fear. And then the teachers were dismissed, and the council workers, and the doctors. There was talk of killings in our district. People we did not know. We were told if we waited patiently it would pass.

Then there were bodies in the street, bodies that were not bodies but messages, warnings, and we were told to walk past them, around them, over them, when we walked into the

159

city. It was forbidden to help. It was forbidden to bury the dead. We carried on. The schools and sports halls became mortuaries, a temporary measure, they said. It was too late to leave by then. We turned our eyes away from the bodies in the street because we had to.

Illy still had work and we needed that. There were no longer classes at the university but he still had to go. It changed him. He said we needed to make our voices heard, do what we could. I didn't want to know. I didn't want to think of him being in danger. Then one day Illy came home in the afternoon, which he had never done before, and told me we must leave. He would not explain why, but we had to leave, right then. There was no time to pack bags, no time to prepare. I was to walk to his brother's house and not to stop until I arrived. He made me run almost. He went away then, back into the city. And I did as he said. The clothes I was wearing. That was all I took. I went with nothing. Do you understand?

Wren nods though she does not want to. Though she has waited to hear this story her whole life, now it is here, she wants to cover her ears. She wants to ask Cleo to stop now, but she knows there is no stopping her.

We were at his brother's house for a week. We heard nothing more. Things were quieter where his brother lived. The fighting seemed to have calmed down. Illy went out each day to support the students and his brother and his brother's wife continued to go to work too.

I had nothing there and I just wanted to get one change of clothes. I would be an hour, maybe two. It was only a mile, less than half an hour.

When I got there, there was no one in our street. It was like we had never left. The house was empty and I let myself in and found the bag I was looking for beneath the bed I shared with Illy. I was collecting some clothes when I heard the front door open. Footsteps on the stairs. Boots. He wore a mask. He carried a gun, though he did not point it at me. I thought he would go, that he would leave me there. I thought that he would turn and go away. Even then. But he took off the gun and put it down on the bed and picked me up off the floor and threw me onto the bed with the gun. And when he was finished I thought that would be the end. He went away. And when he came back there were five of them with him. Five men with boots and black masks. It never seemed to end. They took it in turns and when they left me I think it was because they thought I was dead. I don't remember them leaving, only that the house went quiet and then it was night. It was one bag. One bag.

She says all this in the same quiet voice that does not break or falter. Wren can think of nothing to say. She has never heard her mother talk in so much depth, not about the past nor about anything else but she has no words of consolation for her, nothing to offer.

They sit in silence then, for how long Wren could not say.

And me?

I was pregnant with you when I left O. I didn't know it. I didn't go to see a doctor, not after that. I just wanted to be away from here.

But what about the photograph?

Wren takes the crumpled photograph of her father from her jacket pocket.

That is Illy, yes. He is not your father, though. He should have been. Maybe in another life he could have been. But afterwards, after I told him what I could of what happened,

161

I could not touch him. I could not have him touch me. He didn't understand. How could he understand? We will not talk of this, he said to me. And he would not have mentioned it again. He wanted to un-know it but I could see he was disgusted by me.

He and his brother paid to get me out of the city. It was the only thing he could do. He organised everything, transport, protection. She laughs a little at the word protection.

Wren takes the photograph back.

Illy felt it was his fault, though it had nothing to do with him. It wasn't reprisal or retribution. It was. She pauses. It was what it was. I was angry. I was angry at him, at O, at the war, the whole fucking thing. I wish we'd never come back.

Why did you?

It was nineteen years ago, Wren. A lifetime. I thought I could face it.

And Ariadne?

What about Ariadne?

What about her?

I want to know about her. Why did you keep her?

I promised to keep her safe, she says. I said I'd return her when I came back, but I never planned to return. I needed the money. I tried to sell her in Paris, and again in Amsterdam, but I was told she was worthless. By then I knew I was pregnant with you. I decided to keep her and to keep you, too. I used to think of her when I looked at you. That serious mouth.

I did not think I would play again, but when I got back to my parents, I found the only time I didn't think about O, about what happened here, was when I was playing. It saved me.

162

Wren looks up to see if Cleo is crying but she is emotion-less, at least on the surface. She has relayed the story as though she queued it up years ago in the knowledge she would have to tell it at some point but never managed to find the right time. The result is now it sounds as though the story is playing itself through her, rather than being told. It sounds disembodied somehow. This should change everything. They have never talked like this before, Wren and her mother. They have never talked openly, plainly. She reels from it, from everything she has heard.

She wants to reach out, to put her arms around her mother and, when she does, Cleo submits to the embrace.

I am not ready to leave, Wren says. I need time.

You know they will shut the borders again? she says. I can't stay with you here.

Cleo pays for a taxi for her back to Zamésche. She writes down her new address and presses it into Wren's hand.

The bugs to which we have access are sub-optimal, we tell our superiors. Recordings are often inaudible and that – combined with our illegible handwriting – makes even the most zealous of us wonder about the effectiveness of our craft. So it ever has been.

Still, on this night, when Cleo tells Wren what she has to tell, do we – consciously or unconsciously – nudge the settings on our receivers so that we cannot quite hear the conversation to which we are supposed to be listening? Do the voices sound to us – even those of us who have been commended for our skills in languages – as though they are slightly transposed, so we can discern the voices but not make sense of what is being said? Certainly there is a higher-than-average rate of technical failure on this night for which there is no clear explanation. Do we simply forget to alert the authorities that Wren will shortly leave by the stage door where, despite the small crowd of autograph hunters, they will be able to pick her up easily?

We who have spent our lives dissembling do exactly that. We employ against them the tricks our employers taught us, a collective denial. The truth is that in the absences in our reports, in the blanks between the established facts, we are guilty of a collective forgetfulness that was as little coordinated as it was sanctioned. Is it any wonder we do not want to hear what our fathers and brothers, what we ourselves did during the war? We who, on the anniversary of the official ceasefire – the fighting, the looting, the rapes and assaults continued beyond this date, we know this – are named for the service we offered to O.

Our reports, which are often fabrications, in part or in full, are blank when it comes to Wren Lithgow. We must tell our paymasters what they expect to hear. But somehow we, collectively and individually, do not mention Wren in our reports, so when her photograph appears and spreads like wildfire throughout the city and beyond our borders, she seems to come from nowhere. How can this be? we are asked. But they are not the only ones who are upset. We are distraught that our secret is out. Some of us feel the shame of schoolboys who have been caught spying on a neighbour who sunbathes naked in her yard.

What do you know of her? we are asked. What do we really know of anyone? This is what we do not answer. How can we possibly know anything of her? We do not say these things. We offer up what scant knowledge we have of her activities: when she arrived, where she has been, with whom we have observed her talking, the places she has frequented. We do not say that we feel that something in our souls recognises something in hers. We barely even admit this to ourselves. Yet it is true. She is strange but she is not a stranger to us. She is the daughter who was lost and who has returned to us.

TWENTY

S HE CAN BARELY breathe, barely think. The whole
city seems to slide from under her. Should she have fore-
seen this? Has she always suspected that there was something
wrong? She does not know herself any longer.

Her map, her explorations, all of them seem tainted.
She tastes ash on her tongue. In the washrooms of a bar on
Intriastriste, two streets from the concert hall, she is sick. She
retches again and again until she is empty.

She weaves through the streets and, when she arrives back
at the Porazha, she remembers nothing of the journey, nothing
of the decisions she made, neither lefts nor rights, nor anyone
she had to stop and ask for directions.

Are you all right? Letzsena asks as Wren staggers through
the reception. Do you want me to tell the girls you are ill
tonight?

But she cannot reply. She waves the question away. In her
room, she stares at herself in the mirror. Was she mistaken
that she had seen Illy Donietz-husj's features as her own? Was
that how self-suggestion worked? And what of the soldiers? If
she could peer beneath their tinted visors would she see her
own face staring back in one of theirs? Did their actions haunt
them as they did her mother?

The van winds through the city and until they enter the square
Wren does not notice that they are pulling up in front of the

Kesibyr. They enter the square through a passageway that cuts through two buildings, on a tiled road that is one of the markers of the city. The tower itself is surrounded by a temporary metal fence about two metres tall. As they park, the driver, who is mostly silent, begins to talk. About how the tower is a sign that O is capable of remaking its position among the great cities of Europe. He is hopeful, he says. It is a sign of change, of investment.

The Kesibyr is vast in comparison to the buildings around it, though it would be dwarfed if it was put alongside those that are rising in other cities. Wren does not say this to the driver. It feels to her as if, in this building, the city is testing principles that have long since been found wanting elsewhere.

The area in which the new building stands was once a large open square, the driver says, as he parks the van. The stonework on the floor of the square is arranged in complex patterns that are entirely out of keeping with the tower and the building site around it. In the centre, dances were held, he says, and those who did not dance sat at tables that spilled out of cafes and watched the spinning figures. The cafes are gone now. A supervisor walks to one of the closed gates, produces a key, unlocks the padlock and holds the gate open. There seems to be no one else on the building site as they approach and as doors slide open onto a cavernous entrance hall clad in stone with the appearance of marbled milk. The doors close behind them, their sound as conspicuously designed as the rest of the building. The women's footsteps resound in the lobby and bounce back from the marble walls. There is a folding chair set out against one of the walls but no sign of a security guard.

The supervisors hand out the workplans and the cleaners disperse. Several stop in the hallway and look hopefully towards the lifts, though Wren can see no lights on the arrow boards and she veers off through a doorway to the right of the stairs. The doors between the stairwell and each floor have not yet been hung and she looks into each of the floors as she passes. When she reaches the third floor, the one she has been allocated to clean, she leaves the stairwell, though now she is here she realises she has no intention of cleaning this place. She might never return and there will be no better chance to do the thing she has thought of doing so many times since she arrived in O. There is no sign of anyone else here. The size of the space is unnerving, the uninterrupted expanse of floor space. The silence here is all but complete, the air within trapped behind thick glass. Wires and junction boxes hang from the ceilings waiting to be attached to lights, alarms, cameras. She presumes interior walls will be erected at some point but for now the different offices are marked out in a dull patchwork of carpets and tiling. Though she sees no one else, she can hear people working out in the corridors or on other floors of the building, plumbers or electricians putting finishing touches to the executive suites. She hears systems being fired up, heating or air conditioning, though they stay on for no longer than a few seconds at a time. There is a low buzzing here too, barely perceptible but constant in the background and, though she moves through the offices, pulling the vacuum cleaner behind her, it remains a low-level and constant soundtrack.

Close to one window on the third floor she finds a camera set up on a tripod. There is no sign of the photographer. She immediately thinks of Alexis, though why would he be there? She approaches and looks out of the window. The office on which the camera is trained is empty. It is of a style more typical of what she has come to think of as old O, glazed tiles, ornate brickwork. She walks back across the huge floor and follows the carpeted strips that lead between the areas marked out for offices. Back in the stairwell she resumes her climb.

She avoids the next few floors, from which she can hear the sound of the other cleaners and, further up the building, where she can see no carpets have yet been laid on the floors she passes, her steps kick up dust, fine white particles that will settle again once she has left. There are no windows in the stairwell and the shaft is lit by bulkhead lights that look as though they would belong more happily on a ship. Wren loses count of the floors and when she emerges on the top floor she finds the building is more unfinished here, its skeleton of metal beams exposed. She steps over coils of wiring, offcuts, tools. She approaches one of the huge panels of glass and has to supress a scream when she sees there is someone else there already. It is the driver. He is standing with his forehead resting against the glass. He turns for a moment then goes back to staring out of the window.

This building is the end of O as it was, he says. Do you see? This view will change the way all of us see this place. We have been waiting for this change for years.

The city is in darkness, though as Wren looks out, she begins to make out features, the shapes of buildings in the distance.

She is transfixed by this scene and, as she watches, the city becomes clearer. The moon crowns from behind layers of cloud and as this light stretches across the land the building in which they stand begins to feel to her like a descendant of the great Egyptian pyramids, a place in which the dead look out and exert an uneasy influence over the living. Alexis was right, from here she can see way out to the edge of O towards the mountains of the interior and across the point at which the city gives way to agricultural land for as far as she can see, the grassland a patchwork ocean. The moonlight sets the city ablaze. The numerous bridges that emerge from the glowing mist look like rungs on a rope ladder that have been laid without care across the city, which winds and twists back on itself. The buildings are crammed onto the islands that both the mist and these waterways create. It has not occurred to her before that this is how the city is. From up here, she can see the many ways in which O's countless streets and water-ways curl around each other, eels gleaming and shifting in the bottom of a bucket. The tower swings like an upturned pendulum; the city swims in front of her.

Wren takes in as much as she can, but the sense of vertigo is intense and, after a minute or so, she finds she has to look away. She has stayed far longer than she intended and when she looks around she sees the driver has gone. She turns back towards the staircase and sees the light board above the lift doors is blinking. She presses the call button with no expectation that anything will come of it and watches the blinking light as it climbs. She wonders for a moment if it will be safe to ride in a lift that was not working only minutes before and as the doors open she looks at the empty lift carriage and holds her hand out to prevent the doors from closing again. Inside, the light in the lift pulsates. Wren pushes the button for the ground floor. No response. The first, second, sixth, fifth. She jabs buttons until the doors close and wonders again how wise it is to get into a lift that is, in all likelihood, still under construction.

The movement is smooth, though, like a ferry gliding in a vertical sea on a long swell, and when the doors open she realises she has bypassed the third floor and the ground floor too. She emerges into a cavernous space. She has not considered the possibility of floors below ground level before. It does not seem to make sense that they would build down as well as up here given how tall the building is, how much space there is to fill already. It occurs to her too how great a feat of engineering this is, to build a room so large below the water level in a city that is run through so completely with watercourses. It is warmer down here than in the rest of the building and, instead of getting back into the lift with its pulsating lights, she walks into the dullness of the room beyond and waits for her eyes to adjust.

This room could be from a different building entirely, one that has been in use for years. There are large round tables and covered chairs and the room looks to have been set out for an event and it feels utterly incongruent with the unfinished penthouse from which she arrived. There are tables laid out cabaret style. They are littered with glasses, thick cotton napkins and dirty plates from which the smell of cold food rises. The tables fan out from a raised stage area on which there is a heap of clothing and a headpiece with horns like those of a bull.

Thick carpet absorbs the sound of her shoes and it is not until she comes closer to the stage that she hears someone is playing a piano. The music is so soft that the pedal clicks and the slight creak of the stool are clearer than the notes themselves. When she locates the pianist in the dim light, she sees it is a woman sitting with her back to her, at the keyboard of a grand piano. For a second she thinks it is Cleo, though this woman is much younger. She seems to be playing entirely for herself and Wren wonders if she is preparing for a concert.

The pianist falters and Wren thinks for a moment that the woman has heard her approach, though she does not turn and instead retraces her tracks on the sheet music in front of her and starts the passage over. She is wearing a dark backless dress with a high collar and a scarf that rests on shoulder blades accentuated by shadow and she seems entirely lost in the music. The music, or some quality within it, is familiar. It is a piece Wren has heard her mother playing, perhaps, though the longer she listens the less sure she is. It is complex, discord drifting to melody and back into discord, gently swelling crescendos that lead to modulations on a theme she cannot quite grasp. She moves closer, picking her way between the chairs until she can hear that the woman is vocalising the piano part as she plays, so quietly that it is little more than melodic breathing. She moves to look at the woman side on as she continues to play. Wren is struck then with the sense that she has crossed some threshold for which she has not been prepared.

The music now seems horribly discordant and she feels dizzy and sick and she has the sudden impression that something terrible has happened here. She turns and runs across the room back towards the stairwell and takes the stairs back up to the ground floor of the building.

As she emerges into the dead space of the reception she feels relieved. Part of her had expected that she would find herself in another place entirely. She waits until her breathing slows and the worst of the dizziness has subsided. A diffused light illuminates the reception area from an emergency exit sign, though as she approaches the doors, it looks as though the moon has been covered over by cloud again. The darkness seems all but complete. Her dizziness returns. She needs air more than she needs an explanation for what has happened and she lurches towards the doors, though they do not slide open as they did earlier.

Eventually she finds a side door with an emergency bar that gives when she pushes it. She blinks and as she does she sees, in negative, the image of the pianist in the room beneath the tower and she knows she has seen something that she ought not to have.

Wren runs from the tower though the van is still in the square, the driver dozing in one of the back seats. She runs headlong into the darkness, mindless of the curfew. She needs to be away from it, away from here and now, though even as she runs from the Kesibyr she feels she is heading deeper still into O. At times the buildings seem to gather overhead, blocking out the oblique light from the stars, and the darkness becomes so thick that she can see no way forward at all and she has to trust that if she continues to walk her feet will continue to find solid ground beneath them. She feels watched from every dark corner. She is sweating, cold and hot running through her body, and if she carries on this way, running blind, she will end up in the Meret, the capricious Meret that washes away the chemicals from our factories and cleans our clothes and is drunk by rich and poor alike, and which has an undertow like you wouldn't believe. But she does not make it as far as the river. She trips on an uneven stone, or a metal divot embedded in the pavement, and is sent flying to where she comes to a dead stop, a metre from the riverbank.

TWENTY-ONE

WREN FALLS IN and out of dreams in which she watches her mother pursued by faceless men through the streets of O. She wants to call out directions, to help her mother, but she can't. Her next memory is of the sensation of air on her face and when she opens her eyes she finds she is looking up at a ceiling fan that is not moving, though the lights around it seem to spin. It sounds to her as though there is someone in the corner of the room who she cannot see from the bed and, later, when she can focus again, she sees the source of the sighing noise, a large machine about the size of a photocopier.

At first she finds she cannot move much and she sleeps again and when she comes round she pushes herself backwards against the metal bedframe to sit up. Her head throbs and when she raises her hand to it she finds her head is bandaged. A passing doctor pushes her back to a lying position as if she is not awake at all. The doctor takes her pulse, looks at the screen by the side of her bed and makes notes on a clipboard. Wren tries to speak but her mouth is dry and unresponsive, and the doctor ignores her and moves away.

What happened to me? she asks when the next two doctors arrive. Have I been here long?

One doctor speaks, slowly and carefully in *O'chian* and, while she can make out the words, she can make no sense of what the woman is saying to her. Her words are water. She holds up a hand for the doctor to stop and tries her question again. The two doctors confer for a while, and though they seem sympathetic, she senses they are excited too, professionally interested. She recalls the warning about the hospital. She needs to leave, though the sensation of tiredness is still overwhelming, and she sleeps again and wakes several times to find different people standing over her. She is prodded, shushed and treated like a small child up past her bedtime. One doctor lifts the bandage on her head and the pain is intense. She is aware of blood being taken, her drip being adjusted, and on one occasion she wakes to a man standing over her bed. He looks familiar somehow but when she looks again the man has gone. Most of the time, though, she is left alone. Occasionally, she can smell food in the corridor and is overtaken by a sensation of intense hunger, though the food cart does not stop at her room. The machine in the corner continues to sigh. She loses all sense of time and on each occasion that she wakes it takes her some while to remember where she is.

The hospital sounds like a factory floor. Throughout the day doctors and nurses hold loud conferences outside her door. Orderlies argue and wheel beds up and down the corridor and there is the sound of machines being fired up in other rooms, though they sound to her more like office machines than anything medical.

After a while it seems the doctors have lost interest in her and she swings her legs out of the bed. There is water on a small table but no glass and she drinks straight from the plastic jug. Most of her clothes are missing but she does not suppose that matters and she pulls her coat on over the thin hospital gown. In the hallway, she waits until she can no longer hear voices. From beneath a plastic chair outside one of the consulting rooms, she picks up a hat that looks to have been discarded. It is a man's hat – she does not know this, but it is my hat, left in a moment of carelessness – and when she tries it on, pulling it down gingerly over the bandage, she finds it is about the right fit. She catches sight of herself in the reflection in the glass pane on one of the swing doors and she is pleased with the look. It is like looking at another person entirely. The corridors are brightly lit and empty and though she expects at any minute to be called back to the room, she passes no one on the way to the entrance.

Outside there is a wind blowing through the square which cuts through the coat and the thin gown and is almost enough to send her back inside though she pushes on and loses herself in O until she rediscovers the Porazha, though how many hours this takes she has no recollection.

She knows, even before she pushes open the door to the Porazha, that something is wrong. The square is too quiet. No barking dogs or children scrabbling round the edges, no huddles sharing gossip.

Inside, the reception area is empty. The two television screens, silent and slightly out of sync, show a gameshow but the desk is empty. The whole place feels different. She waits and listens. She is tempted to turn around and leave and not look back, though where would she go?

She walks in a daze through the building. The doors to most of the rooms she passes are ajar and within some she can see disarray, upturned cupboards, turned-out drawers. There is no sound at all aside from the pigeons that live in the netting outside. She is unsurprised to find her own door open too. The doorframe is splintered, the door itself barely holding on. Like the others she has passed on the way up, her room has been turned over, the contents of her drawers thrown around the room, her map no longer on the wall.

She only just makes it to the sink in the corner in time to vomit. The sickness goes on for some time as she brings up everything that is in her system and when the vomiting eventually subsides she is left with the sensation that there is really very little of her left at all.

She manages to crawl over to the mattress on the floor and under the sheets and when she wakes her head buzzes constantly. She is listless, her thoughts dark as the Meret.

She looks again at the wall. The map has not just been ripped down. The whole thing, all its constituent parts, is gone. It is as though it has been removed forensically. There is no sign now that it was ever there, no fragments of it stamped into the floor with her belongings.

Now, time seems to collapse in on itself. The world is light one minute and dark the next. She feels cast away, islanded within the city. Hours seemed to go by in minutes and she finds herself at the window staring out at the city, though with no memory of getting there, and without memory of the impulse that must have taken her from the bed to the window. She can feel her wound is infected and though she is not aware of anyone else in the building, it sometimes sounds to her as though the Porazha is now populated by travellers who have reached some great terminus and are shouting in their own languages, trying to get home or get away. As in the hospital, she can understand the individual words but not the meaning. These panicked voices threaten to drown out a more distant voice that is attempting to calm the crowds, to direct them to where they need to be so that she can find some peace again.

TWENTY-TWO

WHEN SHE COMES to, she is exhausted but the fever has passed. She searches through her clothes, rummages through them as she did in the covered market, until she finds what she is looking for. Whoever turned the room over has taken her passport, the few papers she has, though they have left the little money she had hidden in the pages of the magazines. She finds Ariadne, too, buried beneath a coat in the corner of the room, an overlooked, plain thing. Wren changes into the best clothes she has and puts Ariadne in her pocket.

If it was Wren they came for, they will be back, she figures. And now she has nowhere to go, nowhere else to turn. She could throw herself through the doors of the newly opened embassy, though she knows instinctively that she will be intercepted long before she gets there. Word will have got out of the hospital by now. There is nothing for it. She takes her coat and bag and walks down to the reception to wait for whatever is coming to her. She sits in the middle of the cavernous room. She can hear her own breath and she looks up to see she is sitting beneath a dome, like the one in the library. She had not noticed it before. Sure enough, she finds she is able to hear all the sounds of the room and the sound from the square beyond the Porazha's door, as though it is all being concentrated into this space. She sits and listens to the sound of metal on metal, instruments, loud voices, and it takes her a few minutes to work out they are preparing for the Parade of Lights, setting up stages, putting up fencing along the roads. At least now she will hear when someone is coming.

She drags a chair to the centre of the empty reception. There is nothing left to do. If they, whoever they are, do not come for her, she will leave. She will find a way out of O and find her mother again. She will return Ariadne to Passhau. He deserves to have her. Ariadne belongs here. Wren is all gone to the Meret as we say in O.

She takes Ariadne out of the bag, unhooks the key from its chain. She winds her seven rotations, sets her down on the floor and returns to the chair. Ariadne pauses a moment, turns and begins her movement.

Wren watches Ariadne turn, move, turn, move. When Ariadne stops, Wren steps down from the chair, winds her and sets her going again from the same point. She winds, watches, winds and watches and, as she does, she begins to see branches of rivers emerge, fountains, the shapes of buildings she recognises, the arc of the tramway.

She runs to the reception desk, takes a stick of chalk with which Letzsena wrote her Back Soon notes on the board behind the desk, and returns to Ariadne. She moves the chair to the side and places Ariadne in the centre where the chair had been.

She winds her again and this time, when she sets off, Wren follows her with the chalk, directly onto the floor. When she stops, she winds her again. The city unfolds itself as Ariadne lets out her thread. Occasionally, Wren stops to retrieve more chalk from the desk but aside from these short interruptions she works without stopping. Wren follows Ariadne's path for so long she loses track of time. The wind-up girl turns and turns again, crosses over her own path, doubles back on herself. She moves quickly, efficiently, and if Wren were not so sure of her now, she would think this too was a further form of madness, but this time she is sure. In time, Ariadne comes to the edge of the room where furniture is stacked and Wren clears everything to one end to make more room. Ariadne moves about the space as though she is engaged in a matter of utmost seriousness. She is assured, calm. Alexis was wrong. The Daughter of O was not lost, she was exploring. She was learning the city. She was mapping the unmappable. Eventually, Ariadne returns to the point at which Wren started her, in the centre of the room. Wren's whole body aches from following her for so long. Now, the white floor is criss-crossed with chalk. Wren drags the chair back to the centre point and stands on it. Looking down, she is back in the Kesibyr. She sees the branches of the Meret, spreading themselves throughout the city and flooding out into the sea. She sees Hereckl, Zamésche, Omyr, Erlotz, Symic, the docks and station, the whole city laid out in front of her. The streets appear to twist and turn in on themselves, as though they are moving, but the image is complete. The whole of O contained within a doll. With the exception of Passhau, she is, for a moment, the only person in O who knows what she knows and, before she leaves, Wren takes a bucket of water and sluices it over the chalk-covered floor.

They are waiting for her outside. The authorities, the watchers, Alexis, others whose functions she cannot guess at. If she stays long enough they will come in for her. She would rather meet them on her own terms.

TWENTY-THREE

T HE WIND BUILDS throughout the day, though it is noticed only by those who, on the evening of the parade, go up onto the rooftops to watch.

The streets are emptied of cars and trams, tables are taken from the street into the interiors of cafes and shutters pulled down and, towards evening, the streets become lined with groups gathered around their creations. Outside in the square, groups with tubas, cornets, other brass instruments, sit in huddles. Wren slips on her coat, puts the figure of Ariadne into her pocket and walks out of the Porazha's doors. She whispers a silent goodbye to the building as she stands at the top of the steps for a moment in full view.

An image comes to me unbidden as I watch her, a memory of Wren on the rooftop of Alexis's apartment block in Hereckl, with her rescued bird. One minute there and the next gone, absorbed back into the city. She stands for a moment, looking out at the crowds milling around, and then she descends into streets that are crowded far beyond their capacity.

She looks for signs that anyone recognises her in the mass heading east through the city but everyone seems to be caught up in their own worlds now. As far as she can see, she will be the only person in the crowded streets who is carrying neither a lantern nor an instrument, and she wonders if she is the closest to what might be considered an audience for this festival in which everyone is the show itself. The building wind is noticed. Lanterns are lowered to street level to avoid them being caught in a gust or ripped before they are lit. The carriers of the larger lanterns, the ones that require four or five people to manoeuvre, eye them nervously, as though the lanterns are horses ready to bolt.

She cannot identify what causes the momentary pause but just as it seems the streets can become no fuller, the noise level in the city dips. O seems to freeze, as if this small pause marks the moment that daily life can be forgotten. Conversations stall and stay stalled, instruments are hushed.

We are all waiting.

For the curfew bell. The one night in the year when the bell can be ignored, it will signal something else instead.

It is only when the curfew bell rings that the spell is broken and a roar goes up across the city. As the bell rings, as has been planned and prepared for months, the paper veils from the lanterns are drawn back and the lamps within them lit. From where the road dips Wren watches as illuminated shapes emerge far into the city. As each wave of the parade takes its cue from those behind it the city takes on a new glow, a light more beautiful than any she has known so far. The road that stretches down towards the river becomes a stream of bobbing lights, swaying on a tide of people. There are lanterns that depict wolves, foxes, dragons, that seem to have their own life glowing within them. There are ambiguous forms, boats, trains, whales, bi-planes and jellyfish, tigers, all held aloft above the musicians who march in blocks between the sections of the parade. And snakes, articulated by several hands, and a huge horned creature that towers over the rest and looks to be on the verge of collapse. This creature seems to Wren to be in pain, buffeted in the wind. And on the Meret there are more lights on the boats and the barges and on small rafts. There are fish above water, boats on top of boats.

For a moment it is as if they are one enormous organism and then, when the drums start up, an animal emerging from hibernation. The parade starts to move, at first in short, jerky movements and then in longer pulses until they are walking more or less freely, though tightly packed in the streets. It is beyond the control of one person now.

And among these lanterns are hundreds that look alike, each one a re-creation of the Daughter of O. Hundreds of Daughters of O spread out across the whole city, in front of the press and the dignitaries, the television cameras. They are all recognisable, though there are as many different versions of her as there are lanterns, as worker, as mother, as daughter, as pregnant, her head held high, and within her distended belly is suspended a smaller model, a foetus curled in on itself. They are beyond beautiful and Wren senses that she is watching an act that is somehow sacred.

The procession moves slowly, the rhythms from the different bands of drummers achieving synchronicity and syncopating with the movements of the paper lanterns. The noise is overwhelming. The carriers struggle to keep control of their lanterns in the wind, which now seems to want to free them.

They are closing in, uniformed and plain-clothes police.

Unencumbered, Wren walks between the lantern holders, lost in the noise, for it is noise rather than music now, the marching music and the jazz and the samba bands, and it sounds as though the whole event might have been organised to drive something away, rather than to be a celebration. Rivers of lights stretch out around her like burning threads. She runs with the crowds and feels herself swept along with them. She is embraced, carried along with it and, beautiful though the lanterns are, she watches the faces of those who carry them, their eyes lifted towards their creations, lit by the glow of the candles within.

The wind lifts again and brings with it rain. The rain turns the lanterns translucent then transparent. They take on the appearance of glass and the delicate structures threaten to fold in on themselves under the weight of water, though if anything the intensity of the lights from the lanterns increases. The intensity of the drumming increases too as though in competition with the rain and the fire and the roar of the crowds. A heavy gust catches the wings of an enormous paper bi-plane that lifts itself free of its carriers and soars up, a soaking, burning emblem. What unity there had been for those few minutes in which the streets of O moved as one is broken and the current of the crowd shifts. There is something else aside from the rain that is driving people too, a sort of anger and thickness in the crowd, an anger that Wren did not notice before and she realises that she is caught in something far larger than she expected. She is borne along with the mass of people surging through the city, flotsam in the tide and there seems to be little difference between the rain-soaked air, the rain-soaked street and the river, which every now and then comes into view.

The lanterns are constructed in such a way that they can stand on their own, and as the police approach them, they find there is no one carrying these paper women with fire inside and we film and record the police wrestling with them, trying to move them and drawing more attention to these solemn-faced, accusatory Daughters of O. Several papers and news programmes will report on the attempted arrest of numerous paper lanterns and O's authorities will rail against the traitors who leaked footage to the assorted press.

Elsewhere in O other fires resist the rain, fox fires that the police chase only to find when they arrive that the sources of the fires have shifted and are now in the street beyond or the street beyond that. There are fires everywhere. They spring up all over the city. Fire crews and police units rush to extinguish them, though when they arrive they find the blazes have moved on. They are no longer in the place they were first seen but in the next street on. Police units blunder from street to street, often having to turn back on themselves as they meet dead ends they forgot were there. The air is full of the sound of panic.

The crowds now run to avoid the collapsing lanterns, which are burning and soaking at the same time, soaring through the streets, free of their carriers, uncontrolled and uncontrollable. The marching bands disperse and the rush of people in their varied costumes, to which there now seems to be no theme, no coherence, look like refugees from all the world's carnivals, running from some gross atrocity. Even those who have been the standard bearers look lost, like soldiers detached from their units and divisions.

The darkness, when it eventually falls, is all but total and the rain falls heavily on the metal roofs of the kiosks in the streets, on the roofs of the houseboats in the river too, and people walk as though blindfolded. In the chaos, the lanterns flying up into the air and the fires and the noise, she can make sense of nothing and it is at this point she feels a hand take her own in the darkness. It is the hand of a young girl, and she knows it is hers, the hand of the Daughter of O. It is the hand she has been waiting to hold for so many years now and it leads Wren away. She marvels at how natural it feels, their fingers intertwined, as if they have been holding hands for years.

ACKNOWLEDGEMENTS

I WOULD LIKE to thank the following people, who were a great help to me in writing this novel: Nicholas Royle, not only for insightful editing but for shooting the cover photograph that has now become, for me, *the* photograph of Wren Lithgow, Bella Royle for modelling for the cover, and John Oakey for the excellent design; the team at Salt Publishing for their passion and commitment; Peter Straus and Eliza Plowden at Rogers, Coleridge and White for advice and guidance; Arts Council England for awarding me a grant that enabled me to take time out to write; Amy Lilwall, Kerry Hadley-Pryce and Alasdair Menmuir, for close reading and considered comments; Stephen Kelman, Ann Sansom, Rachel Joyce, Katy Mahood, Craig Barr-Green, Jennifer Young, Jay Armstrong, Carys Bray, and Chelsey Flood for kind words and encouragement at just the right time; Cathy Rentzenbrink for walks, talks and good advice; the late, great Bill Mitchell, who offered much-needed advice when I first conceived of the idea for the novel; my colleagues and friends at Falmouth University's School of Writing and Journalism, and the team at The Writers' Block, Cornwall; Bec Evans and Chris Smith for walks in the woods; Mum and Maurice, Dad and Alison for unswerving support. In particular, I would like to thank Liz Jensen for her ongoing belief, for insightful reading and for spurring me on.

I owe a debt of thanks to Kate Eichhorn, whose book, *Adjusted Margins, Xerography, Art and Activism in the Late Twentieth Century*, inspired the depiction of the student activists at the Porazha, and to Nicolas Iljine, whose *Odessa Memories* provided the inspiration behind Alexis's anecdote about the Greek statue. Georg Simmel's essay, 'The Metropolis and Mental Life', and Zygmunt Bauman's *Liquid Modernity* both helped in my development of O.

And most of all, my thanks and love to Emma, Alana and Tom Menmuir.

This book has been typeset by
SART PUBLISHING LIMITED
using Mrs Eaves, a font designed by Suggi Isuzu
for the Mecanic Type Foundry in the Czech Republic.
It is manufactured more than ten Books trust set
House Stewardship Council™ certified paper from the
Hoberg paper Mill in Sweden. It was printed and bound
by River Limited in Bungay, Suffolk, Great Britain.

CROMER
GREAT BRITAIN
MMXIX

This book has been typeset by
SALT PUBLISHING LIMITED
using Neacademia, a font designed by Sergei Egorov
for the Rosetta Type Foundry in the Czech Republic. It
is manufactured using Holmen Book Cream 70gsm, a
Forest Stewardship Council™ certified paper from the
Hallsta Paper Mill in Sweden. It was printed and bound
by Clays Limited in Bungay, Suffolk, Great Britain.

CROMER
GREAT BRITAIN
MMXIX